GLYNDŴR

SON·OF·PROPHECY

I Delyth

Er cof annwyl am
Moelwyn Jones (1943–2015)

GLYNDŴR

SON·OF·PROPHECY

MOELWYN JONES

With grateful thanks to my family:
Dylan, Bethan, Ffion, Gwennan and Catrin,
and also to my wonderful friend, Iris Cobbe,
for all their support.

Delyth Jones

First impression: 2016
Second impression: 2018
© Moelwyn Jones family & Y Lolfa Cyf., 2016

Cover illustration: Teresa Jenellen

ISBN: 978 1 78461 300 6

Published and printed in Wales
on paper from well-maintained forests by
Y Lolfa Cyf., Talybont, Ceredigion SY24 5HE
e-mail ylolfa@ylolfa.com
website www.ylolfa.com
tel 01970 832 304
fax 832 782

1

IN THE EARLY hours of Good Friday, the first day of April 1401, Thomas Easton, a carpenter of the coastal town of Conwy, awoke. The satisfying slumber of a hard-working artisan had been rudely broken and each second of returning consciousness brought a wild, gut-jerking fear as understanding of his terrifying predicament struck home. He tried to cry out but a hand was clapped roughly against his mouth, stifling the sound. He struggled despairingly to disengage the powerful arm wrapped around his upper body, but to no effect. Another surge of terror coursed through him as he felt a hard metal point pressed firmly against his neck.

'Do you wish to live to see the dawn breaking, Master Easton?'

The words were spoken softly, almost casually, but the timbre of the voice was firm and the tone cold, displaying a lack of emotion which the carpenter found chilling. In that moment of paralysing fear he foolishly tried to turn his head towards the speaker and immediately squealed in shock as the sharp point of the blade was pressed harder into his neck. The cold metal punctured the skin, releasing a sudden, warm flow of blood which dribbled down his neck and onto his chest.

'Now you listen to me, Thomas Easton.' The whispered words failed to hide a broad but cultured Welsh accent, which did nothing to ease the carpenter's fears. Welshmen were not allowed inside the borough of Conwy after dark, and were certainly not allowed to bear arms at any time.

'My name is Rhys ap Tudur and Gwilym, who is sitting on your legs, is my brother. We have important business at the castle this morning and we need a little assistance from you to make our visit a success. After that, you will be free to go and we will not harm you. But we must be able to rely on you for a short while, Master Tom. I warn you that any attempt to escape or to impede our activities, in any way, will result in your instant and certain death. Is that clear to you? If it is, nod your head and I will release my hold. Be mindful of my warning though, for human life hangs on the lightest of threads and can be ended very swiftly.'

For the first time since his ordeal had begun, Thomas Easton felt a glimmer of relief and the hope that there might still be a chance of survival. Whatever nefarious activities the Welshmen had in mind seemed to be totally dependent on his active co-operation. It would not profit them to kill him unless he were foolish enough to raise the alarm or attempt to escape. Thomas was a reluctant hero, and self-preservation was still possible if he did as he was told.

'Do you have any small beer in the house?' asked Rhys ap Tudur as he released the man and rose slowly.

'Y… yes… yes… of course.' Thomas's voice was hoarse and his throat painfully dry. 'I will get some from the kitchen.'

'No. You will stay there.' Gwilym ap Tudur spoke for the first time, his tone sharp and determined.

Watching the man leave the chamber, Thomas realised that the brothers were very different. Rhys was older by some years. He was short and strong and certainly not a man to be taken lightly. Despite his blunt threats, the Englishman had the impression that Rhys was a reasonable man, thoughtful even, and not given to impetuous action. Gwilym, by contrast, was quite tall, younger and slimmer, but also a hard, tough-looking man. He would be much more likely to be led by his emotions rather than his brain. Rhys was definitely the man in charge, and that was a relief to Thomas who felt that he was marginally safer with the elder brother in control. As long as he co-operated with them, Rhys would keep their side of the bargain and set him free at some stage.

Gwilym soon returned with three tankards of small beer on a wooden tray.

'Get dressed in your workaday clothes,' Rhys instructed Thomas. 'And get your tool bag ready. As I am to be your apprentice today, I shall carry the tool bag.' He smiled faintly at the stunned look on the carpenter's face.

For a while the three men sat at a small table by the window, watching the enormous bulk of Conwy castle slowly emerging from the morning mist as dawn broke. Conwy was one of a chain of formidable castles, built by the English King Edward I to keep the Welsh in check following the defeat and death of Llywelyn ap Gruffudd, the last native Prince of Wales, in 1282. This castle was one of the most majestic of those structures and considered impregnable.

Rhys took a contemplative sip of his beer. 'My friends tell me that you, Thomas, have been working inside the castle every day for the past fortnight.'

'That is true, my lord. I was first called to repair the great table in the banqueting hall – a job which took us most of the first week to complete as it had been very rudely used. It would have been easier to build a new table,' he added ruefully. 'After that the Constable kept discovering other tables, chairs and bed frames in need of repair. I finished last night though, so I am free to carry out any carpentry you may desire.'

The brothers exchanged a quick grin before Rhys responded. 'We require none of your carpentry skills,

Master Thomas. All we want you to do is a little play-acting.'

Rhys paced the room and stood at the window once again. 'This is what we need, so listen carefully. Soon, the Constable, John Massy, will lead his entire garrison, except for a few token guards, probably – to the parish church to attend the Good Friday service. Once they have departed, you, the carpenter the guards are used to seeing every day, accompanied by me, your faithful, temporary apprentice, will walk across the drawbridge and knock on the great door. When challenged, you will tell the guard that you are reporting for work, as usual. If he wonders why you are working on Good Friday you will say that you have one extra job to take care of which must be finished by tomorrow. If he should ask where your regular apprentice is, you will tell him that the young man's mother is very devout and will not allow him to work on the Lord's Day. I am simply a friend who has agreed to help you out. All we need is for the guard to let us in. That is all. Your task will be over and you will be free to leave.'

Thomas stared at him open-mouthed. 'B… bu… but this is madness! Such a ruse will never fool the guard. And what if we do manage to get inside, what happens then? We will be cut down as soon as they realise they've been tricked.'

Rhys grabbed him roughly by the shoulder. 'Believe

me, it will work – as soon as that door swings open, Gwilym will lead a company of two score armed men across the drawbridge to aid us.'

'You intend to take the castle and hold it with just forty men?' Thomas's face was etched in disbelief.

'Indeed we do, my English friend. A castle with defences like this could be held against an army of many thousands with a garrison of forty trained and well armed men. The current defenders, who may shortly be caring for their souls instead of guarding Bolingbroke's castle, are not such a great host, surely?'

'Well no, I suppose not, less than a hundred I should think,' Thomas speculated.

Gwilym laughed. 'Our friends tell us that the garrison has thirty-four archers and thirty men-at-arms. Would you say that is an accurate assessment, master carpenter?' he enquired mockingly.

For a moment Thomas could not hide his irritation. 'Who are these friends of yours, and how is it that they seem to know everything?'

'No self-respecting commander would expect his troops to attempt to capture a castle without knowing what they were up against. So, he needs to ensure that he has accurate information. That is why I have informants among the servants within the castle. Some are English. There are always those who wish to earn some easy beer money. They are happy to supply me with information, for a fee, secure in their belief that the castle is impregnable. Others are Welsh servants who provide the information for nothing, though no-one goes unrewarded. They are used to verify the facts provided by their more senior English colleagues.'

'How is it that a hard-working, upstanding burgess like you is living on your own?' Gwilym asked, suddenly changing the subject. 'Have you no wish to marry and raise a family?' Thomas turned quickly towards the window, but not before the brothers had seen the desolation in his eyes.

'I was married once. We lived in Chester and we were blessed with a son and a daughter.' There was silence for a moment and the Welshmen realised that the carpenter was re-living an old sadness.

'They all died of the Plague... within days of each other...' his voice tailed off.

'I am sorry,' Gwilym said quietly, his voice sounding almost gentle.

'That's why I came here. Too many bad memories in Chester. It has been four years now and not a day passes when I don't think of Mary and the children...'

'You have our sincere sympathy, Master Thomas,' said Rhys. Then more brusquely he added, 'But we have pressing business to attend to, and we will not let our sympathy stop us from carrying out our threat if you do not follow our instructions to the letter. Do as we say, and you will be unharmed and free to go as soon as I set foot inside that castle.'

'You will have no trouble from me, believe me. I want to live,' Thomas responded hurriedly.

The three settled again around the little table by the window. There was an air of expectant tension in the room as they sat quietly, waiting for the soldiers of the garrison to emerge from the castle. After what seemed like an age, the great doors swung open and the portcullis was raised, its weight causing the stout iron chains of the lifting gear to squeal in protest. There was a flurry of shouted orders and a thin, bearded rider emerged, seated on an impeccably groomed black destrier, followed on foot by a company of men-at-arms, with a company of archers bringing up the rear. Few, if any, of Conwy's burgesses saw the procession as the garrison made its way down the quiet street towards the parish church, for most were still in their beds.

Rhys laughed as he saw the carpenter's puzzlement. 'Have you not heard of cousin Owain? No, I don't suppose many of the good citizens of Conwy have heard of him… yet. Never mind. Soon, Master Thomas, you and your fellow burgesses here, and throughout Wales, will come to know Owain ap Gruffudd Fychan ap Gruffudd, also known as Owain Glyndŵr. Since last September, we Welsh serve him as our Prince. He is none other than the Prince of Wales, and what we do this day we do in his name.'

As Rhys reached the end of his speech he and Gwilym stood stiffly to attention, each with a hand resting on the hilt of a short sword at his belt.

'It is time to give Bolingbroke the shock of his life. We have had little success since the initial declaration of Owain as Prince of Wales, in Glyndyfrdwy, last year. Bolingbroke must think that the would-be rebellion has been thoroughly quashed. Indeed, he must be convinced it was just a rather ridiculous charade. And what fool Owain for choosing the life of an outlaw over his previously comfortable existence as Lord of Sycharth and Glyndyfrdwy with a family, lands and a measure of wealth. Well, the usurper who calls himself King Henry IV must be made to understand that no-one trifles with Owain Glyndŵr, and we are not quite the fools he takes us for.'

Rhys was suddenly the image of steely resolve. 'Gwilym, go and ready the men, but make sure that they are well hidden from the castle guards until Thomas and I are safely inside. Then, bring them over that drawbridge at the gallop.'

The younger brother was on his feet in an instant and reaching for the door. 'Good luck,' he whispered as he left, carefully sidling along the wall of a neighbouring house before disappearing around a corner.

'Well, Thomas, now it is just you and me. Both our lives are in your hands and, believe me, if you make the wrong choice out there – you will be dead before I am.' Rhys spoke with a cold conviction which Thomas found unnerving. 'Be a good lad though, and this will be a very good day for the two of us.'

The moment for action had arrived and the carpenter felt weak at the knees as a gnawing fear began to eat at his insides. He watched Rhys ap Tudur lift the tool bag over his shoulder, seemingly with little effort, and forced his legs to move in order to follow the Welshman out of the house. Once out in the street, Rhys instructed him to take the lead and to walk with his usual gait as they crossed the drawbridge.

'Turn to me occasionally. Make pretence of chatting normally,' said Rhys, adjusting the tool bag so as to hide the sword hanging from his belt.

The short walk across the drawbridge seemed never-ending and there was no sign of Gwilym and his men. On reaching the castle entrance Thomas turned to Rhys for a signal, then grasped the large, heavy ring in the iron-studded door and gave it several hard knocks. There was no immediate response and Thomas, his stomach tied in knots, breathed heavily, silently cursing his weakness. Rhys stood patiently, balanced on the balls of his feet and, unbelievably, gave the fearful carpenter a reassuring wink!

After several minutes they heard footsteps. Someone was approaching from the gatehouse guardroom. Inside the great door, a smaller door designed to allow entry to people on foot, opened slowly and a portly armed guard stood there, filling the aperture. He made no effort to hide his boredom as he yawned loudly. He seemed on the point of asking them what their business was when everything moved very swiftly. Rhys's bunched fist shot out, striking the yawning guard hard in the mouth. The man careered backwards, blood pouring from his mouth, and sat down with a bump several feet away. Rhys shoved a startled Thomas aside and sprang through the open door. Thomas had a partial view of the guard struggling to stand up, swearing and spitting broken teeth, only to be hit again, even harder, by Rhys on the jaw. This time he went down and lay still.

'Thomas, come and help me open the main door, then jump out of the way – my gang of ruffians are upon us…'

The carpenter spun around and saw a horde of loud, yelling men in green jerkins, waving a variety of weapons – swords, pikes, axes and bows – charging across the drawbridge. Hurriedly, he helped Rhys heave the heavy door open. Within seconds they were all inside, shouting triumphantly, while a small group began to unfurl a large red dragon banner.

The guard had regained consciousness but decided to remain prone in the face of overwhelming odds. He was suddenly hauled roughly to his feet by Gwilym and bundled over to where Rhys was preparing to address the men. As Rhys raised his hand for silence, half a dozen more men in green jerkins raced across the drawbridge. Their leader came to a halt in front of his lord, breathing heavily.

'The town has been fired as you instructed, my lord… and… I… we have just seen the Constable leading his men from the church at the double.'

'Very well. Let us raise the drawbridge, close the great doors and lower the portcullis. Archers, man the ramparts, string your longbows but wait for my command before taking any action against the English. Thomas, are you still here? You have seconds left to run across that drawbridge…'

'My lord, I beg you, let me stay here with you. If I run now, and the Constable sees me, I will surely be tortured and hanged as a collaborator. Also, you may well need my carpentry skills. I can tell you that the drawbridge will not budge, for it has not been raised in living memory, and must be thoroughly seized up.' Thomas's face was a study in desperation.

'You have served me well this day. And, you have a point, we may need a skilled carpenter in the coming days and weeks,' said Rhys, after a brief hesitation. 'As for the drawbridge, it does not really matter. The great doors are stout and that formidable iron portcullis would keep any force at bay, even if the enemy could get passed a hail of arrows.'

Turning his attention to the cowering guard and the men-at-arms awaiting instructions, he shouted, 'Release this man and let him take his chances with his unhappy Constable – quickly, before the portcullis is lowered…'

Eager hands helped the unfortunate guard onto the drawbridge seconds before the portcullis came rushing down, clanging into its defensive position as soon as the heavy, iron-studded doors had been closed. Thomas had a fleeting glimpse of John Massy, the castle Constable, cantering up to the far end of the drawbridge followed at the run by his men.

'I believe there is one other guard hiding somewhere within the castle,' Rhys spoke urgently to his men. 'I want that man found as soon as possible. Tread very carefully, just in case he wants to play the hero. You will conduct the search in pairs and keep either in view, or within hearing of each other, at all times. Meanwhile, I will join the bowmen on the ramparts. Massy will, no doubt, want to parley. He needs his castle restored before news of its capture reaches Bolingbroke. Remember, I want all the castle's servants treated with respect. Many of them are our own countrymen and women anyway, and who knows for how long we may need their services.'

Rhys turned to his captain, Gerwyn Dal. 'Organise your men in pairs, Gerwyn, and start searching for that guard.'

The tall, bearded captain began issuing crisp orders to his men while Rhys turned on his heels and headed for the nearest tower to find a stairway up to the ramparts.

Thomas, left to his own devices, went and sat on the cold flagstones and leaned against the castle wall, still bewildered by the speed of the morning's events and their fateful implications for him. There was no way he could continue living a normal life as a carpenter in this borough, after helping the Welsh raiders capture Conwy castle. The fact that he had done so under duress would have no bearing on the matter, as Massy searched desperately for any scapegoat to face the consequences of his own failure to safeguard the castle. Yet Thomas's position with the raiders was still unclear and full of danger. To most of them he was still just an English carpenter – a 'tame enemy', nothing more. He was quickly brought out of his reverie by shouting high up on the castle walls.

Rhys and Gwilym ap Tudur stared with undisguised pleasure at the town below them engulfed in flames, with many of the wood-built artisans' homes blazing fiercely. Much closer, near the entrance to the drawbridge, John Massy and a small retinue glared up at them, their anger apparent in their shouts and gestures. The Constable had obviously sent the bulk of his force to help the townspeople to fight the fire. Rhys held up his hand as a signal to gain Massy's attention and waited for the shouting below to die away.

The Constable gritted his teeth. 'What is the meaning of this lawlessness, Welshman? Your action this day is one of high treason against the King of England. For taking possession of this castle by foul trickery and burning the houses and workplaces of the honest burgesses of Conwy, you will be put to death. I shall personally see to it that you suffer most horribly before death claims you.'

'I find your words as illogical as they are stupid, Englishman,' Rhys retorted. 'You seem to have forgotten one basic fact. You are in Wales, not in England, so how can any action I take be construed as an act of high treason when I answer to my sovereign lord, Owain, Prince of Wales, and not the usurper, Henry Bolingbroke, or to anyone who happens to sit upon the throne of England? As for putting us to death, beware Englishman, it would take only one arrow from any of my archers, and you would be a dead man. Indeed, you may soon be killed by an English hand, as official punishment for allowing a small band of Welshmen to take your castle from under your nose.'

'A curse on your rebellious tongue, Welshman. I am sending a messenger to Henry Percy in Chester, the King's governor of north Wales, to report on your vile deeds. Rest assured, he will be here in days with a large host. We will retake the castle and deal with all of you.' With that, Massy turned his horse's head and rode away.

'It will be a pleasure to do battle with the famous Hotspur,' Rhys shouted after him. 'At least we will be fighting a seasoned warrior whose competence is not in question, unlike our present sorry adversary.'

The Welsh leader descended the south-east tower's spiral staircase and called to his brother. 'Gwilym, I want a short meeting with yourself, Gerwyn Dal and Meurig ap Siôn, the archers' leader, in the great hall. Bring Master Easton with you too.'

Gwilym laughed. 'Well brother, you certainly got the better of the battle of words with Massy. I would not wish to be in his shoes when he meets Hotspur to explain how he allowed this massive fortress to be taken without so much as a single weapon drawn.'

By lunchtime the little town of Conwy was a scene of devastation. Lives had not been lost, for Rhys's men had herded the townspeople into the main square before firing the buildings. Now, with most of the fires extinguished, the wrecked town was a small collection of roofless stone buildings, with the charred remains of the predominantly wood-built neighbourhood still smouldering and filling the air with noxious fumes.

In the castle's great hall a small group huddled around the high table in conference. The second guard had still not been found. Rhys instructed his lieutenants to ensure that every nook and cranny, including the servants' quarters, be thoroughly searched again. Other than finding the elusive soldier, the immediate priority was to discover the state of food supplies and weaponry. Large quantities of both would be required to withstand a siege.

'We will be best served if we can keep the besiegers at long range, so the most pressing requirement is a good supply of arrows. We will need far more than we managed to bring with us if we are to dissuade the enemy from attempting to breach the walls,' Rhys mused. 'Food, of course, will be absolutely vital. We know that the castle has a monthly delivery of staple foods from Chester, as well as small numbers of live sheep and pigs from the surrounding countryside, to provide a steady supply of meat. But there is little space, even in a castle of this size, to keep large numbers of animals. There is no grazing, of course, so the animals, too, have to be fed. We need to check the state of the most recent delivery and talk to whoever runs the kitchens to establish the food situation. I entrust that task to you, Gwilym.'

Rhys's eyes roved around the table and settled on Thomas the carpenter.

'Have you any experience of fashioning arrows, Master Thomas?'

'I served as fletcher and bowyer with the Earl of Arundel's retinue in the naval victory over the French in 1387, my lord,' Thomas replied. 'I can fashion an arrow as well as any man – and a longbow for that matter...'

'Good. Then you can search the armoury and elsewhere for suitable materials. In addition to sets of bows and arrows, shipments of weaponry usually include arrow heads, feathered fletches and suitable elm staves for making both longbows and arrows. There may even be some imported Spanish yew in store.'

Shortly afterwards, Rhys closed the meeting and dismissed the men in order to make his own inspection of Conwy castle. As his companions filed out of the hall he noted, with satisfaction, the pleased look on Thomas Easton's face. The carpenter had been given an important task to fulfil and Rhys's senior aides had been present to witness their leader's trust in the Englishman, something which was bound to improve his level of acceptance amongst them. Thomas was already beginning to feel better about the whole situation.

That night, the capture of Conwy castle was celebrated with a magnificent feast in the great hall. For one night everyone, including the servants, was encouraged to relax and enjoy the celebration of the triumphant and daring occupation of the castle by the small band of Anglesey men. Sentry duty on the battlements was entrusted to twelve volunteers split into two watches, who had been promised a feast of their own the following evening and an extra day free of duties. It was a decision which more than a few of them secretly regretted when the delicious aroma of pig roast wafted up to them as they paced the battlements, staring down at the pitiful remains of the town, now largely empty. Most of the inhabitants had left to stay with friends and relatives in the safety of other English boroughs on the north Wales coast and its immediate hinterland.

Rhys and Gwilym ap Tudur, seated at the head of the high table, looked confident and relaxed. The castle had been captured with even greater ease than they had anticipated. The brothers had great pleasure in imagining the excitement and acclaim which would be sweeping through north Wales and beyond, giving fresh heart to Owain Glyndŵr and his hard-pressed rebels. It would be particularly welcome to those rebels whose initial encounters with professional English forces had been less than successful. During one debacle, Glyndŵr himself had only just managed to evade capture. Now, the loss of Conwy castle would have shocked and horrified the English authorities, for they had always believed that the ring of castles erected by Edward I more than a hundred years earlier was impregnable. Indeed anyone who had seen the mighty castle at Conwy, with its eight defensive towers and soaring curtain walls, would undoubtedly have agreed. Its reputation had now been severely dented, as had the notion that the English military machine was invincible. The fact that this Welsh success had been achieved by stealth rather than force of arms would have turned the garrison, and particularly its commander, into incompetent figures of fun. The King and Parliament would be furious, and that was a most satisfying thought for the feasting Welshmen in the great hall.

Another, more immediate, cause of satisfaction was that the missing guard had been discovered, cowering under the bed of one of the maids. Rhys and Gwilym had decided to keep him prisoner for the time being, on the grounds that he might be a useful source of information during the inevitable negotiations which would, eventually, have to be conducted with Henry Percy.

There had been very good news on the provisions

front. They had estimated a supply of up to eight weeks of food and ale at normal consumption levels, which could be stretched to almost three months with the introduction of moderate rationing. Arms were also in good supply, while Thomas had found ample materials for making longbows and arrows. The garrison had obviously relied on existing weapons for many years with no apparent thought given to fashioning new ones. Thomas had petitioned Rhys for likely volunteers from among the archers for training as fletchers. One difficulty would be communication, because Thomas spoke no Welsh and the majority of the Welsh bowmen had little or no grasp of English. Rhys had reassured him that Meurig ap Siôn, their leader, spoke English fluently and would act as translator, at least until someone else could be found.

The following morning, most of the little band within the castle awoke with sore heads but with warm memories of the previous evening. It was late morning when a messenger from John Massy arrived at the gatehouse. The erstwhile Constable wanted an audience with the leader of the Welsh invaders. He wished to set up a parley, supported by two aides, all unarmed. He also wished to know the Welsh leader's name so that he might address him with civility.

Rhys and Gwilym glanced at each other in some amusement on hearing this.

'You may tell the former Constable,' Rhys stressed the word 'former' and paused theatrically while Gwilym quietly stifled a guffaw, '… that he may safely attend an audience with Rhys and Gwilym ap Tudur, nobles of the island of Anglesey, and that the rules of chivalry will apply. I suggest we organise a private dinner in the Constable's office this evening for, say, the hour of eight. Any weapons will, in any event, be confiscated by the gatehouse guards and returned to their owners on departure.'

The brothers conferred for some time after dismissing the messenger, deciding on tactics for the evening's verbal confrontation with John Massy and his small delegation. It was agreed that the whole tenor of the meeting would reflect the fact that they, and not Massy, were now in full charge of the castle. The opportunity would be seized to impress upon the English visitors that the Welsh rebel band was intent on holding on to it for some time, with every confidence in their ability to do so.

2

A LOG FIRE burned brightly in the large fireplace in the Constable's office. Servants were putting the finishing touches to dressing the long table, which took up almost the whole length of one wall of the large chamber. It had served as office and briefing room to every Constable of Conwy castle since it was built by Edward I, more than a century before. Rhys had decided to match the numbers of the English delegation by asking Gwilym and Gerwyn Dal to join him. He had also decided to cement his position as the new commander of the castle, the man holding all the advantages, by initially sitting behind the desk, with his two delegates on either side of him. Massy and his delegation would sit on plain wooden chairs in front of the desk as supplicants. The introductory discussion would take place over a pre-dinner glass of wine before the six moved over to the table for the meal. Once again, Rhys would occupy the chair at the head of the table with his two lieutenants on either side, nearest to him.

The English delegation arrived at the castle entrance shortly before eight. They were searched for weapons, before being escorted by the duty officer to the meeting chamber. John Massy entered briskly, unceremoniously elbowing the officer aside. His two companions entered more deferentially. The three behind the desk rose politely, Rhys allowing a small scowl of displeasure to register with Massy, before smiling broadly.

'Ah, Massy, thank you for joining us. You and your companions are most welcome.'

The English officer came to a halt in front of the desk, the others flanking him but one step behind. He was obviously struggling to control his temper as the significance of Rhys's positioning struck home.

'I was pleased to grant your request for a face-to-face meeting. It is always good to have discussions with one's adversaries,' Rhys continued smoothly. 'It helps us to understand one another's position, including both sides' ambitions and intentions in a given situation.'

Massy breathed heavily, making a real effort to swallow his pride as he recognised the condescension in the Welshman's voice. He realised that the whole scene was intended to show him who was master of the situation. He was also intelligent enough to recognise that the man's effrontery was calculated to annoy him, so that he would not be able to conduct their discussions with a cool, analytical mind.

'As Constable of this castle my message to you, Master ap Tudur, is a simple one. Yours is a course of action which can only have one conclusion. It is simply a matter of time before the castle will be back in English hands. It is merely a question of when it will happen. Now, as I have said before, occupying this castle is an act of high treason, punishable by death. However, Henry Percy has asked me to inform you that if you show immediate contrition for that unlawful act, then our new King, Henry IV, may be persuaded to show clemency – a free pardon even – for you and your brother and, possibly, for some of your men. That would, of course, be dependent upon you relinquishing the castle to me within the next twenty-four hours.'

Rhys's smile never wavered, though Gwilym's face darkened in anger, while Gerwyn Dal stared in disbelief at Massy.

'As I said Master Massy, talking through any situation helps each side to understand the other, and to realise what the other side's limits of tolerance are when negotiating a solution. However,' and Rhys's voice assumed a steely tone as he continued, 'any discussion must be based on the reality of the situation. It seems to me, sire, that you have not yet caught up with the reality of this one.' His voice dropped almost to a whisper but each word came across very clearly. 'You are not here as the Constable – but as the former Constable. You are now in the presence of your successor and, as Constable, I would advise you to approach the evening's discussions on that basis. Now, let each side make every effort to continue with civility rather than threats. May I offer each of you some wine and do, please, be seated.'

With curt nods of the head to his two companions Massy sat down on one of the small wooden chairs facing the desk, the other two taking their places on either side.

'Well, I suppose we had better begin with introductions.' Massy's voice sounded resigned and deflated. 'On my right is my personal secretary, John Fellows. He will be taking notes as required during the meeting.'

Rhys turned his attention to the secretary for the first time. He saw a thin, sallow-faced young man, prematurely balding, with pale blue, watery eyes which blinked rapidly every few seconds. As he inclined his head in greeting, Rhys examined the young man carefully, trying to gauge any strengths or weaknesses. The immediate impression John Fellows made was one of an inexperienced, nervous young man. Rhys, however, was too experienced a campaigner to form an instant opinion and decided to note the youngster's every comment during the evening, and weigh them with care.

'My other colleague may be a surprising one in your eyes. You would do well, though, to start looking at the world through his eyes and taking note of the benefits that loyalty to the Crown can bring. He is a countryman of yours – I give you Gwilym ap Gruffudd, one of the foremost Welshmen in north Wales.'

Rhys's nod was almost imperceptible as he stared coldly at the man introduced so enthusiastically by Massy.

'Bradwr…!' The unexpected interruption by Gerwyn Dal came as a surprise to everyone and made the Welshman in the English delegation start in sudden fear as the Welsh word for 'traitor' was spat out with some venom by the big officer.

Rhys held up a cautionary hand and the tension visibly left Gerwyn's formidable frame as he subsided once again into his seat.

'Indeed Master Massy, Gwilym ap Gruffudd is a man known to all of us on this side of the desk, but it is the first time we have met. I must confess I do not understand what advantages he brings to this meeting, but if he has constructive comments to offer, we will listen.'

Rhys spoke frostily, not taking his eyes away from Gwilym ap Gruffudd. For his part, the short, portly subject of Rhys's stare shifted uncomfortably, his eyes darting back and fore at the three men behind the desk. Gwilym ap Tudur had a face like thunder while Gerwyn Dal stared steadily at the ceiling as if unwilling to recognise the man's existence.

Rhys cleared his throat and turned to Massy. 'Very well. I am Rhys ap Tudur and this is my brother Gwilym, on my right. The other member of our delegation is Gerwyn Dal, my captain. Now, let us move on to more formal discussions at table.'

There was a scraping of chairs on the flagstone floor as everyone rose and followed Rhys to the table. He took his place at its head, his two companions seated next to him on either side. Massy pretended not to notice the slight and sat next to Gwilym ap Tudur.

'You are a very self-effacing man, my lord,' Massy smiled thinly. 'My Welsh companion has told me a great deal about you and the historically important position of your family in this area. Your lineage is, apparently, a splendid one. You two are descendants of Ednyfed Vyckan, chief minister to Llywelyn the Great, Prince of Gwyneth. Your family has produced many of the most influential men in north Wales for the past century and a half. You, Rhys, were the Sheriff of Anglesey until King Richard II was deposed in 1398. Also, you and your brother have led detachments of troops to France and to Ireland in the King's name. Like Master ap Gruffudd here, you learned to co-operate happily with the English authorities in Wales. And, dare I say it, you have profited greatly from that co-operation.'

Massy paused, enjoying the irritation and discomfiture on the faces of his hosts. 'All of which begs the question, gentlemen – why?' He stretched out his arms in a theatrical gesture of incomprehension. 'Why would the highly respected ap Tudur brothers of Penmynydd, Anglesey, one a former royally appointed Sheriff of the English Crown, and both of whom having served as ranking officers, with distinction, in English armies in France and Ireland... why would they turn their backs on all that to take part in a hopeless Welsh rebellion? This short rebellion is already in its death throes and you all face the real prospect of being hanged, drawn and quartered, leaving your dependents totally destitute. Where is the sense in that?'

There was a short, tense silence.

'Is that question being asked simply to try and annoy us or are you seriously seeking a proper answer? I ask because the answer will not be a brief one and will require your full attention for some while.'

'Sire, a serious answer would be of great interest and, I can assure you, will get my full attention.' Massy's response was couched in polite words but a faint smirk still hovered on his lips.

Rhys composed himself for a moment then began speaking slowly, and clearly, as if addressing a child.

'In your English eyes – we are the Welsh. But we are only "the Welsh" to the English. As I understand it, the word "Welsh" means "strangers". We, the Britons, inhabited what are now known as Wales and England for centuries, living as a civilised society with our own laws, customs and traditions long before the English nation was born. When you did invade Britain you were no more than a collection of heathen tribes – the Angles, the Saxons, and Jutes. You conquered all the rich, flat agricultural lands by force of arms and by dint of sheer numbers, pushing us westward to the mountains and moorlands of Wales (the land of strangers). I find your reference to us, the people whose lands you stole, as the Welsh, a breathtaking example of supreme arrogance. So England was born. Your state was still in its infancy when you, in turn, were conquered by the Normans and your language heavily influenced by Norman French.'

Rhys, pausing for a draught of ale, noted with satisfaction that his words were clearly ruffling English feathers, for both Massy and young Fellows were looking decidedly piqued.

'We, however, are the Cymry, the people with common interest, the people with close ties, bound together by language, a wealth of history and, above all, a long and proud heritage. We are a people who honour bards as much as we honour heroes and mighty warriors, and we discovered a very long time ago that words are often more powerful than the sword. Our country is Cymru and our language, Cymraeg. We are a proud people, Massy, and even after more than a hundred years we find it difficult to accept the idea of being a conquered race. We often console ourselves with the memory of ancient prophecies handed down through the generations by poets, who are held in very high esteem. Apart from composing fine literature and recording the deeds of our ancestors, they remind us of the prophecies of the prophet Merlin (or Myrddin as we call him), who foresaw that we would one day recover the lands we once held. As for the ap Tudur family, we belong to the surviving class of Welsh nobility, the Uchelwyr. This class consists of descendants of former princes and chieftains who still exercise a great deal of influence and authority over their compatriots. Each family of Uchelwyr has its own plaid, or clan, to call upon for support when needed. You ask why my family decided to bow the knee and give service to the English Crown?'

Rhys paused for a moment. 'The fact is – it was our only means of survival. After the death of Llywelyn the Last in 1282, murdered in a cowardly ambush while travelling to an agreed meeting with the English, the Uchelwyr had to choose between swearing fealty to Edward I, being executed for treason in the most barbaric manner, or starving to death after being deprived of all their land. Each King, in turn, increases taxation, while the Marcher Lords pounce on every excuse to extort money from tenants who, in any case, are often made homeless by the greed of those tyrants.

Add to that the ravages of the Black Death over the last thirty years and we no longer have enough hands to produce sufficient food for ourselves, let alone food to sell. Any produce we do have to sell has to be sold to English people in the boroughs, who pay us a pittance with smug smiles on their faces. I could go on to describe how English law makes sure that we are very much second rate citizens in our own country, with no rights of redress against English wrongdoers, but I won't, because you know all that well enough. So, why are we here embroiled in rebellion? I and many others, Uchelwyr like me, are convinced that in Owain Glyndŵr we have the most credible and charismatic potential saviour of our people since the last Llywelyn.'

Rhys reached for his jug of ale.

'And what has this Glendower done to justify such touching admiration.' The question was asked in a surprisingly crisp voice by the, so far, silent John Fellows. The Welsh delegates stared at him in surprise and they all noticed a marked hostility mixed with disdain in the young man's eyes.

'Good question. It is indeed gratifying that you have found your tongue, Master Fellows,' said Rhys. 'Let us start with his attributes before we go on to his deeds. Owain ap Gruffudd Fychan is the direct male descendant of the princely house of Powys Fadog. This family, founded by Bleddyn ap Cynfyn, ruled north-east and mid Wales as well as areas now within the Marches for generations. On his mother Elen's side, Owain is directly descended from the rulers of Deheubarth, traditional rulers of south-west and parts of south Wales. This is the house of the legendary Lord Rhys and its illustrious founder, Rhys ap Tewdwr. Incidentally, Owain's family and ours are kin as his mother and our foster mother are sisters. He also has some claim of descent from the greatest of the three princely houses, that of Gwynedd. He is certainly the last of the male line of that house. So you see we have, in Glyndŵr, a perfect claimant to the title of Prince of Wales with connections to all the old ruling families of Wales.'

'Sounds good… almost too good to be true,' John Fellows sneered.

'Tell me, Master Massy,' said Gwilym ap Tudur brightly, his voice sounding surprisingly friendly. 'How long has this young man been in Wales?'

'About two months I would say. Why do you ask?'

'Because I can't see him lasting very long if he does not alter his attitude when conversing with Welshmen,' responded Gwilym quietly, giving Fellows a hard look. 'However, I am sure that you have been here long enough, Massy, to understand that if there is one area where the Welsh never get it wrong, it is genealogy. You will no doubt rid the young man of his rough edges, and I would advise you to do it sooner, rather than later.'

'I think this may be a good time to have our meal served,' Rhys broke in to lighten what had suddenly become a tense atmosphere. He quickly rose and, opening the heavy oak door, shouted down the corridor that the company was ready for the meal to be served. The servants had obviously been awaiting the summons, for the corridor immediately echoed to the sound of many feet as a host of servants brought in steaming bowls of meat and vegetables, as well as more ale. Several of the servants passed by Master Massy with heads bowed and eyes averted, obviously nervous in the presence of their former Constable. Massy simply sat there, grim-faced, staring straight ahead while the Welsh delegation pretended not to notice. Finally, everything was ready and the servants left, closing the door behind them, leaving the improbable group of diners to continue with their discussion.

'So, gentlemen, that is the new Prince of Wales. Now let me tell you a little of what he has done in his life...' said Rhys smoothly.

'Well now,' Massy interrupted, 'you have already given us a glowing portrait of Glen...'

'Ah, not so fast Master Massy. It was your wish and that of young Fellows here to know everything about our new leader, and you will hear me out,' Rhys responded firmly.

'Owain Glyndŵr, now in his mid forties, is a very

far-seeing, well travelled, and educated man who, believe me, would not have started this rebellion unless he thought he could succeed in throwing off the English yoke. He is accomplished in the use of weapons and has experience of service in English armies. He is also well known in these parts as a formidable jouster at tournaments. Owain was born in the family home at Sycharth in 1353. He did not have the happiest of childhoods. His father, Gruffudd Fychan, died when he was a young lad and the next few years were difficult ones for Elen, his mother. Gruffudd Fychan had been employed as an estate manager by the Marcher Earl of Arundel. The Earl was kindly disposed towards Elen and took Owain into his own home to be trained as a squire. So, Owain suddenly found himself in a different world, that of the English rulers of the March where language, attitudes and customs were very different from those of the Welsh gentry and bards at Sycharth. His immersion in this new world was to prove a great help to him in understanding English attitudes and furthering his education. A few years later, he was taken into the service of another friendly family of English origins, that of David Hanmer, later Sir David Hanmer. Like many English gentry in the Marches, the Hanmers had mingled with their Welsh counterparts and intermarried. David's mother was Welsh and David himself had married Angharad, daughter of Llywelyn

Ddu ap Gruffudd, one of the most prominent Welsh families in the Chirk area. So both Welsh and English were spoken in the Hanmer household. Like Sycharth, it was often visited by Welsh bards.'

'You obviously regard this Owain as an educated man,' John Fellows interjected. 'Perhaps you can explain to us how he came upon this wonderful education… could it be the work of your famous bards?' The young secretary's voice was loaded with sarcasm.

'Certainly, Master Fellows. David Hanmer was a prominent lawyer who eventually became a Justice of the King's Bench, sitting in judgement in cases brought before the King. He also became a Member of Parliament. Owain certainly received an excellent grounding in the history and literature of the Britons from the bards, Then, while he was still a very young man, David Hanmer enrolled him as a scholar at the Inns of Court in London, where he studied English law and the wider political system, as well as the customs and hierarchical set-up of the Royal Court. In fact he was there for nearly seven years. He became a popular figure at court and got to know Richard, the Boy King, and Henry Bolingbroke, son of John of Gaunt, then but a boy, but who now calls himself King Henry IV. I see from the deflated look on your face, Fellows, that my answer was rather more impressive than you had anticipated.'

'You mentioned earlier that Glendower has considerable experience in the military. I would be interested in more detail of his career as a soldier.' Massy's voice was neutral.

'Well, I can tell you that between 1384 and 1389 he served in the King's armies on several occasions as an officer,' Rhys responded. 'These included service under the famous Sir Gregory Sais in defence of Berwick-on-Tweed against the Scots, and another campaign in Scotland a year later. He was part of the private retinue of the Earl of Arundel in the action against the French, including the victory over the French fleet in the English Channel in 1387. He also took part in the battle of Radcote Bridge, in December of that year. Another consideration, of course, is that all these campaigns gave Owain the opportunity to meet, and get to know, many of the greatest men in England.'

'The man you describe sounds a very formidable opponent and I am glad I asked the question,' said Massy, who seemed genuinely impressed by Rhys's resumé of Owain Glyndŵr's pedigree as a serious threat to English supremacy in Wales.

'The biggest factor in all this, of course, is whether he can inspire his countrymen to rise in sufficient numbers to pose a credible challenge to our authority, and can he do so in every corner of Wales? I have to say, the evidence so far shows nothing of the sort. One thing is certain, he will have to prove himself to be a charismatic leader before the end of this summer, otherwise he and the rebellion will be finished.'

Massy saw from the concerned frowns on the Welsh delegation's faces that his words had struck home. The few military clashes which had taken place since the proclamation of Owain as Prince of Wales had not been very encouraging, and it was rumoured that the Prince had been forced to hide in the mountains during the past winter, accompanied only by a handful of his closest associates. This was the moment to press home his advantage.

'The problem besetting Glendower will also be the problem facing every one of you. How will you be able to escape the King's vengeance and how can you protect your loved ones from his wrath? Would it not be your wisest move now, having gained your moment of glory in capturing this great castle, to seek Henry's pardon? That would save you and your families from the calamity which will surely engulf Glendower, and his few followers, very shortly.'

There was a brief silence, broken by the scraping of a chair as Gerwyn Dal rose to his feet. When he spoke the tone of his deep voice was low and reasonable, with only the fire in his eyes betraying the emotion he was feeling.

'My lords, I am the only common man in this

company, but I represent thousands of ordinary Welshmen who have not even woken up yet to the hopes and dreams which Owain Glyndŵr is offering us. He is the man who will lead us to the same rights and freedoms that all English people take for granted. He is the man who will help us shake off the English yoke and ensure that we rule ourselves and make our own laws, as we used to before the coming of the invader. Let me tell you, Master Massy, Glyndŵr will never be betrayed to the English by a Welshman or woman. As for your King's vengeance I, for one, will take my chances and remind you that you, and others like you, had better beware of facing our Prince's wrath, though I doubt he would inflict cruelty on your loved ones. You see – he is a civilised man, not given to acts of barbarism.'

'Well.' Rhys ap Tudur rose and clapped the huge captain on the back appreciatively. 'There is your answer, Massy. That is the sort of loyalty our cousin enjoys. I don't think you, or Hotspur, or Henry Bolingbroke yet realise the seriousness of Owain's rebellion. He is fighting for a cause which will strike a chord in the hearts of Uchelwyr and ordinary people alike throughout Wales, and it will soon grow into a full-scale, national revolt.'

Both sides realised that an impasse had been reached which would not readily be resolved and the rest of the meal was eaten in relative silence, with Rhys and Massy struggling uncomfortably to make sporadic small talk. The ap Tudur brothers, however, noted the intense hostility in John Fellows' eyes and the almost continuous drumming of his fingers on the table as he finished his meal in silence.

Later, after the English delegation had left, the brothers and Gerwyn Dal stayed on awhile to share their impressions of the evening. All were agreed that Gwilym ap Gruffudd's presence as a member of the English delegation, intended as a means of persuading the Welsh force to abandon the castle, was an act beneath contempt. The man was not worthy of further consideration. Massy, they felt, was a professional English officer, probably efficient in carrying out his day-to-day duties, but not particularly perceptive. Understandably, the man was seething after having allowed the castle to fall into Welsh hands so easily, and so unnecessarily. There would undoubtedly be unpleasant repercussions for him when the King finally decided where the blame for the Welsh coup lay. The big surprise of the evening, though, had been John Fellows.

'If Fellows is Massy's private secretary then I am a horse with two heads,' exclaimed Gwilym ap Tudur with a dismissive shrug of the shoulders.

'A snake in the grass I'd call him,' Gerwyn Dal growled.

Rhys quaffed his ale and carefully wiped his lips with the back of his hand. 'I agree he is certainly no secretary – he did not take a single note all evening, anyway. I also believe he is older than he seems. The boyish looks were certainly not in evidence on the occasions I managed to ruffle his feathers. It would not surprise me if he is Henry's eyes and ears in this area, with the King's personal authority to make Massy's decisions for him, if needs be. Whoever and whatever else he is, he's a nasty, devious little man – someone to be carefully watched, that is for sure.'

In a long, single-storey, stone-built hall only a few hundred yards away from the towering walls of Conwy castle, another meeting was taking place. This building was the administrative centre of the little borough and in a small room at the rear of the hall another three men had gathered for urgent talks. Henry Percy had arrived in Conwy with a mounted escort of forty men a bare half-hour before. He was tired and knew himself to be short tempered due to fatigue and, he had to admit, due to the terse message from the King which had arrived in Chester that morning, and which still seemed to be burning a hole in the leather pouch at his belt. Now he was closeted in this meeting with two men, one of whom he had little faith in and the other whom he distrusted and disliked intensely. The subject of his loathing was a thin, weasel-like young man who now blinked rapidly as their eyes met. The other was John Massy, the man who had been entrusted with the defence of Conwy castle.

Hotspur took a slow mouthful of red wine from his goblet, swilled it around his mouth appreciatively and swallowed, taking his time in order to control his temper and to try and disguise his contempt for the pair.

'Well, gentlemen, I'm sure it will be no surprise for you to hear that news of the fall of Conwy castle has not been greeted with any great enthusiasm in London. On the contrary, the King is furious and Parliament is in a state of shock – panic even.'

Hotspur paused to let his words sink in.

'I have, on my person, a letter from Henry, obviously dictated in a great rage in which he is intent on finding the person or persons responsible for the loss of a great fortress in such an "idiotic manner", his words, and then skinning that person or persons alive!'

'My lord, that is surely unfair.' Massy's face was bright red, whether from embarrassment or anger was not clear. 'It was Good Friday. Good God, even the Welsh must know enough of the rules of chivalry to realise that you do not attack your enemy's possessions while he is at prayer on such a holy day.'

Hotspur sighed deeply. 'Oh for goodness sake, Massy, you don't seriously believe that great leaders win their battles by following the codes of chivalry? Surely a soldier of your experience must know that war is an ugly, messy affair where men kill or get killed, usually in the most brutal fashion, and to achieve victory both sides will employ any means, fair or foul. Men whose backs are against the wall, knowing their loved ones will be in mortal danger if they lose the battle, are not going to pause in the midst of the fight to ponder on whether or not they are following the rules of chivalry! Believe me, you had better come up with a better excuse than that if you wish to keep your head on your shoulders when the King comes to visit…'

Massy glared at Hotspur for a moment, then subsided, his shoulders visibly drooping, his brow glistening with sweat.

Fellows cleared his throat. 'Gentlemen, I see little value in dwelling on culpability in this matter. Surely, the important thing now is to recover this castle as soon as possible, before this Glendower fellow can inspire his rebels to attempt attacks on more of our castles.'

'And how do you propose we do that, Master Fellows?'

'Why, attack of course. You, my lord, have a fighting force of over a thousand men arriving tomorrow. You also have a reputation for decisive action and this is a wonderful opportunity for you to show His Majesty how you can surmount this kind of situation.' Fellows thumped the table with a small fist to emphasise his enthusiasm.

'A wonderful opportunity, eh?' Hotspur smiled tightly and eyed the young man almost pityingly. 'Well, since you are clearly something of an expert on siege tactics perhaps you could elaborate for us on how these rebels could be induced to give up the castle promptly, so that we can hand it back to the King?'

Fellows coloured, his smile swiftly switching to a scowl as he realised that Hotspur was patronising him. 'I am not a soldier, sire, as you well know,' Fellows bridled. 'I just thought that as we shall soon have close on twelve hundred men to their forty, there would be a good chance of overwhelming the defenders through sheer numbers.'

'What you don't say is that each of those "numbers" is a human being,' Massy interrupted indignantly. 'They would die in their scores, in their hundreds even, in that kind of attack and there is no guarantee that we would take the castle, even then.'

'Let me tell you what we do not have,' said Hotspur quietly. 'We do not have siege engines here that could be used to batter the walls. We do not have hundreds of very long siege ladders to scale the walls and I suggest that the majority of those forty defenders know how to use the longbow. I can assure you that Welsh archers are the best, second to none. I can vouch for that because

I have fought alongside them in English armies against the Scots and the French. They will have the cover of the castle walls and the advantage of looking down at us, while our archers will have no defence other than their light armour, and at that short distance there are plenty of places where a well-aimed arrow would be lethal. As Massy says, our casualties would be enormous. In any case, without siege ladders we would have no means of scaling the walls.'

Fellows smiled a nasty little smile. 'I have to say that I am more than a little surprised... and troubled by your negative attitudes...'

'I would call my attitude realistic rather than negative...' Hotspur interrupted sharply.

'Before sending me to these parts,' Fellows continued as if he had not noticed the interruption, 'the King asked me to observe and report back to him as often as required. Among other responsibilities, I was charged with observing the manner in which his officers conducted the suppression of the Welsh rebellion. As part of that particular order, I was told to report any officer, no matter of what rank,' here he paused, eyes glinting triumphantly in Hotspur's direction, 'if I felt that he was giving anything less than his full and most enthusiastic attention to the task in hand.'

In a blur of movement Hotspur was on his feet. His hands reached out like whips and, grabbing Fellows by the throat, he hauled him across the wide oak table so that his face was an inch from his own, with the rest of his body floundering helplessly among the goblets of spilled wine.

'You dare to threaten me?' he roared.

'Have a care, my lord,' Massy said urgently, 'I can understand your rage, but this man, despite his ignorance in military matters does have the ear of the King.'

Massy's placatory words seemed to increase Hotspur's fury. He hauled Fellows bodily across the remaining section of table and shook him like a rat.

'By the gods, do you really think you can frighten me with your childish self-importance? Do you, you little whelp?' With his face turning red as Hotspur's grip tightened around his neck, the King's favourite was in no position to answer. Hotspur shook him again before flinging him against the wall. His light body slammed into the stone wall, his head striking it a split second later with a sickening crack, before he collapsed on to the floor and lay still.

'By all the saints, Percy, you have killed him.'

'No such luck.' Hotspur was leaning on the table, breathing heavily. 'His kind lead a charmed life and I have no doubt he will soon be on his feet again, thinking up devious little schemes to do maximum harm to the Welsh rebels – and to me!' he added with a mirthless grin.

3

THREE DAYS LATER a large group of armed men appeared at the end of the castle drawbridge. At their head was Hotspur in full battle armour accompanied by Massy, also in armour and Fellows in civilian clothes with his head heavily bandaged.

'As I told you, Lord Percy, the King has asked me to confer with you most urgently. It is his wish that an attempt should be made to dislodge the Welsh usurpers from the castle.'

'Have you explained to the King the difficulties of such a course of action and the heavy losses we are likely to incur?' Hotspur was finding it difficult to maintain a civil tone of voice.

'Yes, I explained your position very clearly to His Majesty.'

'Do you know why His Majesty does not issue me, the governor of north Wales, with direct orders in this matter?' Hotspur enquired testily

'I do not, my lord. However, he is most insistent that an attack should be attempted no matter what the cost.'

'Very well,' said Hotspur. 'I have had some two

dozen siege ladders built, though not of the quality one would have wished. Siege engines could not be used even if available for they would cause serious and costly damage to the walls which I am sure the King would not wish.'

As Hotspur turned to issue instructions to his section commanders, there was a shout from the castle ramparts.

'Henry Percy, this is Rhys ap Tudur. You will remember me from campaigns in which we fought side by side. You are one of the few Englishmen I have any respect for. As a former ally I ask you not to carry out your planned attack for your own safety and that of your men. My archers, as you know, are very accurate and we have a plentiful supply of arrows. If you attack there will be carnage and your attack will fail at a huge cost in lives.'

'I hear what you say, Rhys, but I have orders which have to be followed. I appreciate your warning but I am not in a position to heed your advice. Have a care because it may be you who will end up witnessing the carnage of your own men.'

'We both know what is about to happen here. There will be many more widows in England by tonight,' Rhys responded. 'However I realise your predicament, Hotspur. My advice to you would be to place that young rat Fellows at the forefront of the attack and I will ensure that, if you live through this day, your own life will be a lot easier and safer.'

'Your offer is a considerate one, Welshman, one which I am sorely tempted to accept.' Hotspur laughed grimly as he turned to Fellows who was listening to the exchange with growing alarm. Then he turned his horse and walked it back through the lines of armed men to ready his forces for the attack.

Inside the castle, Meurig ap Siôn was issuing final instructions to his archers, while Gerwyn Dal marshalled his men-at-arms along the ramparts ready to throw off the expected siege ladders. Thomas Easton, who had struck up an unlikely friendship with Meurig during their joint venture to manufacture a healthy supply of arrows, was charged with organising piles of arrows in suitable places along the ramparts so that the longbow men could maintain a constant bombardment of the enemy when they commenced their attack.

With everything in readiness, an eerie silence enveloped the castle ramparts. As the minutes passed the defenders began to wonder whether Hotspur would attack after all. Suddenly, a loud blast on a trumpet shattered the silence, startling the Welshmen. Two rows of archers appeared, trotting into position on either side of the drawbridge, leaving a central avenue for the men-at-arms to surge onto the drawbridge when Hotspur issued the command.

Meurig ap Siôn had been waiting for this moment and had primed his men for it. Before the exposed English bowmen could ready themselves, they were enveloped in a murderous hail of arrows which clove large gaps in their ranks. The survivors gamely returned fire before they were caught by another vicious salvo from the castle walls. At a shouted command, the English archers beat a hasty retreat, leaving the area they had occupied strewn with the bodies of dead and wounded. A ragged cheer arose from the castle's defenders before petering out as they stared in disbelief at the scene of horror before them.

Hotspur too stared aghast as wounded men, some screaming in pain, others in shocked silence, crawled and staggered from amongst the dead in search of safety. He was relieved to see that the Welsh made no further attempt to fire at them.

'This is suicide, Percy.' Massy's voice was a mixture of disgust and reproof. 'These men are professional soldiers and will do as you command, but what they are being asked to do here is beyond all reason. Stop the attack now Percy, in the name of God.'

'I am perfectly aware of that,' Hotspur snapped. 'But the King's orders must be obeyed and that unhappy responsibility is mine.'

Abruptly he raised his arm and turning to the waiting men-at-arms he roared the order. 'For England and King Henry, forward!'

From his vantage point high above the gatehouse Rhys ap Tudur saw Hotspur leading a seemingly never-ending body of armoured soldiers in a charge across the drawbridge. Others, many carrying siege ladders, waded across the moat on either side.

'Right, lads. You all know what to do. In the name of Owain Glyndŵr, Prince of Wales by the Grace of God, to your battle stations!'

Again the entire area of the drawbridge was filled with the deadly whistling of arrows in flight, the metallic thud as the arrowheads pierced English armour with ease and the cries of the injured. Welsh longbows, made mainly from elm, were known to be capable of killing a man without armour at three hundred yards and even the best armour was totally useless against them at up to one hundred yards. Some of the lucky ones who managed to reach the walls pressed themselves as close to the hard stone as they could but several were killed, a few taking arrows in the eyes as they looked up at the defenders. Amazingly, some of the attackers still managed to raise their ladders and clamber up towards the Welsh men-at-arms. Most of these were easily dealt with by the defenders who pushed them away before the attackers could climb more than a few rungs. The two or three ladders which were successfully held in place allowed a few of Hotspur's men to reach the battlements but these few struggles were hopelessly unequal as the Welsh soldiers clubbed or stabbed their adversaries so that they fell mortally wounded on top of those climbing up behind them, sending their comrades tumbling also.

In less than half an hour the attack was over, the surviving attackers grateful to get out of range of the murderous longbows. None of the defenders had been injured but the drawbridge and the surrounding area was a scene of carnage with scores of bodies, some piled on top of each other, littering the ground. Later a band of Hotspur's men, unarmed and including a white flag bearer, came to remove the bodies.

Rhys, Gwilym and their followers, though sickened by the day's bloody work, were relieved and jubilant after the successful defence of the castle and relaxed with a well-deserved meal and extra rations of ale in the great hall.

The archers' leader, Meurig ap Siôn, sat with Gerwyn Dal at the high table, discussing the success of their tactics and wondering whether Hotspur would attempt any more direct assaults on the castle. They both agreed that another attack was highly unlikely, indeed it was doubtful whether his men would willingly mount such a suicidal action again.

Gazing around the hall, Meurig's eye fell on Thomas the carpenter eating his meal at the end of one of the long tables. He had come to like the bluff Englishman. He was intelligent, honest, hard working and good company once engaged in conversation. Meurig had also asked Gwen, a fresh-faced serving wench to help him familiarise Tom with the Welsh language. His face now split into a grin as he saw that Gwen was paying an inordinate amount of attention to Thomas, offering him extra helpings of food and drink, leaning close when she spoke to him and always with a smile on her face. He wondered absently whether the conversation was being conducted in Welsh or in English. Looking at them, it occurred to him that the language mattered not a jot. The body language of both required no translation.

Much later that night, Meurig, unable to sleep, stood in the shadow of the east tower, enjoying the mild, moonlit spring night. He thought of his wife, Mair, and their two small sons in Benllech on the island of Anglesey; his gentle Mair, who could be such an exciting lover when aroused. Annoyed at allowing such thoughts to light a fierce stirring in his loins, he shifted impatiently, trying to ignore the longing and the hiraeth. A moment later he saw a shadowy figure emerge from the men's quarters, stepping gingerly towards the building housing the kitchens and various storage chambers. The figure stopped occasionally when a sentry paced the ramparts immediately above him, then continued on his furtive journey, carefully avoiding loose pebbles on his way. Meurig loosened the short sword at his belt and followed his quarry with equal care. Who could it be? Was there a traitor in their midst? And who was the man sneaking out to meet at dead of night? Suddenly the figure stopped and turned to examine the shadows behind him. Meurig paused also. For a fleeting moment Meurig thought that he had been discovered. Then the moonlight lit up the man's face and the archer almost laughed aloud as he recognised Thomas Easton, and his fingers relaxed on the hilt of his sword. Apparently satisfied that he was not being followed, Easton resumed his careful progress, eventually disappearing through a small doorway which Meurig knew led to the storage area close to the kitchens.

Thomas now found himself in total darkness. He remembered how Gwen had described the linen store as the third door on the right along the passageway. His confidence returned as he noticed a small glow of light under the ill-fitting door to his right. Gwen must have lit a candle. Hesitantly he reached for the rusty iron door handle. It turned without a squeak and he eased himself inside wondering whether Gwen might have oiled the latch and lock. Back along the passageway, Meurig ap Siôn saw him disappear into the storeroom and, smiling in delight, he turned and made his way back to his quarters.

'Do you always enter a lady's bedchamber without knocking?' Gwen's voice was low and inviting. Tom peered across and saw that she lay in a makeshift bed, the coverlet hiding her entirely, except for her face with her long brown hair tumbling exotically around it. In the dim yellow glow of the candle Tom thought he had never seen anything so mysteriously beautiful and exciting.

'Only when the lady has invited me,' he responded breathlessly as he began to peel off his clothing.

Gwen blew out the candle and whispered, 'Come to me, my love. It feels as if I have been waiting an age for you.'

Wasting no time Tom climbed in beside her, realising as he did so that she, too, was naked under the sheet. His mind was in turmoil. He had not made love to anyone since his wife's death four years previously, nor had he felt any desire to do so. Now this dalliance with the cheery and attractive Gwen had happened so suddenly and awakened old but powerful desires. It was all the more poignant because she, too, had been widowed some six years before when her husband was killed in Ireland, fighting in King Richard's army. She, also, had almost lost the will to live and had felt no desire to meet another man until now. Tom held her in his arms and kissed her tenderly, his arousal increasing with every moment. She moaned and returned his kisses fiercely, at the same time swinging him around so that he lay on top of her, and spreading her legs so that his lower body sank into a cosy haven of warmth between her thighs. Before he could do anything himself he felt her hand holding him firmly and guiding him inside her. After that, their first coupling was short but fierce as they both raced quickly to an ecstatic climax, releasing their years of pent-up frustration and subconscious need. They lay totally spent, breathing heavily for a while as the wonder of their lovemaking filled them both with languorous contentment.

Gwen was first to turn to look at him. She smiled shyly and said simply, 'That was truly wonderful.'

Tom was almost overwhelmed with a protective tenderness towards her and again he held her and kissed her softly on the mouth. Once again he felt the hot flush of desire which increased sharply as Gwen responded to him eagerly. This time, however, they were both feeling totally relaxed in each other's arms, and now they took their time…

4

THERE WERE NO more direct assaults on Conwy castle but as the days stretched into weeks – then into May, the exultant mood of the defenders began to change. Although they had prevented Hotspur from repossessing the castle, the very nature of the stalemate meant they were prisoners within the stronghold. The English maintained a sound siege so that there was no possibility of even a single defender slipping out unseen. Boredom was the biggest problem. The brothers and their officers kept the men as active as they could with hours of physical exercise and weapons practice every day. Rhys would address his force several times a week reminding them that, as long as they held the castle, they were doing Glyndŵr's cause a power of good by showing how a hugely outnumbered band of determined Welshmen could hold a large English army at bay for weeks, months even. He told them that they were the toast of every patriotic Welsh hearth, rich and poor, throughout the land. However, the monotony of living closely in a confined space for such a long time gradually created a dispirited atmosphere, which affected everyone in varying degrees. Another worrying factor was the uncertainty of what lay ahead. How would it all end? Rhys had introduced food rationing in mid-May and towards the end of the month he was forced to place everyone on half rations.

One day, a message came from Hotspur, requesting a private meeting with Rhys ap Tudur inside the castle. From time to time the two had conducted short, shouted discussions across the drawbridge, but these had never resulted in any positive developments. Rhys responded immediately, promising Hotspur safe conduct and a private meeting in the castle the following morning.

'This little chat with Hotspur could be significant,' Rhys told his officers later that evening.

'Being an experienced campaigner, he must realise that we are running low on provisions and that morale may be slipping a bit. This is an ideal time for him to offer us terms for an orderly return of the castle to his charge, and I look forward to hearing what those terms may be.'

'Well, we know Percy, having campaigned alongside him several times,' Gwilym reflected. 'He is a hard man, but fair. He is also cunning and ambitious. He will want to end this affair with his own reputation enhanced. As he is now in charge of north Wales his aim, I think, would be to deal with us in a chivalrous manner. His task will be a lot easier if he can convince those Welshmen who are not yet won over to our cause that he is a fair and just man who will treat them well, so that there is really no need for this rebellion.'

'I agree,' said Rhys. 'Unfortunately, he may not be allowed to use his diplomatic talents. He is answerable to a vengeful Bolingbroke who may see things in a quite different light.'

After an indifferent spring, the following morning was the first genuine summer's day of 1401. As early as ten o'clock the sun, burning in a cloudless blue sky, made the open areas within the castle oppressive. The sentries on the ramparts clung to any patch of shade the towers afforded them. Behind the castle the Conwy estuary shimmered, the small wavelets offering transient pinpoints of sparkling light in the gentle westerly breeze.

An English trumpeter appeared on the far side of the drawbridge and gave three long blasts on the instrument. Seconds later Henry Percy appeared on a snow-white destrier, his tall frame encased in a long surcoat emblazoned with the Percy coat of arms, an azure lion rampant on a bright yellow background. As he rode the horse at walking pace across the drawbridge, the portcullis was raised and the massive doors opened to admit him. Rhys ap Tudur, standing some twenty paces inside the courtyard, had to admit to himself that the tall wiry man in his brightly coloured surcoat cut a dashing figure. Hotspur dismounted and walked towards him with a broad smile on his face. As he approached the short, burly figure of Rhys he greeted him with respect, having fought at the Welshman's side and knowing him to be a very good man to be alongside in the heat of battle. They shook hands and clapped each other on the shoulders before turning and walking towards the Constable's office, where the parley was to take place.

'Can I offer you some cold small beer or ale from the cellars,' Rhys enquired of his guest as they sat down facing each other, at the long table.

'A cold ale would be just the thing in this heat,' Hotspur responded, grateful that the breeze wafting through the open window made the chamber considerably cooler than the castle courtyard. Rhys called a servant who soon returned with a jug of ale and two pewter tankards. For the next few minutes they talked of old times, remembering where and when they had fought together in King Richard's army. Soon though, the conversation turned to their current predicament as leaders of opposing forces who both badly needed to find a way out of the current impasse.

'Let us speak plain on this, Rhys. You have now occupied this castle for two months, so you must be running low on provisions. You have probably been on half rations now for a couple of weeks and things will get very difficult for you soon, unless you can do a deal with me. Would that be a fairly accurate assumption of your situation?'

Rhys heaved a great sigh and nodded slowly. 'There is no point in denying it. You describe my situation pretty accurately. However, you too, I suspect, are faced with difficulties, though of a different kind. I would guess that you would deal reasonably with us in order to reoccupy the castle and bring the matter to a swift end, if you could. But you are having to please Bolingbroke who is, I would wager, intent on regaining his castle and punishing us harshly for what he sees as our treasonable acts.'

Hotspur grinned briefly then frowned as he drank from his tankard. 'You have described my situation perfectly. I have tried to counsel Henry to treat you gently and to ask Glyndŵr for a list of grievances. My view is that if the King could show the Welsh people that he is prepared to listen to their concerns and make some changes to the new, barbaric laws that he and Parliament have concocted against the Welsh these last months, then whatever Glyndŵr may think, the great majority of his countrymen would be willing to put down their arms. In effect, the rebellion would collapse. But Henry was ever the bull at the gate, and has no subtlety. He insists that anything less than harsh punitive measures would be seen as weakness on his part.'

'Aye, and a short memory,' said Rhys bitterly. 'Did you know that during the great Peasants' Revolt of 1379, Owain spirited the boy Bolingbroke away from the Tower, right under the noses of the rioters, thus saving his worthless life?'

'Did he, by St George! Now that I did not know. And how did Glyndŵr come to be in London on that fateful day?'

'He was attending the Inns of Court at that time, studying English law and getting to know some of the greatest men in England.'

Hotspur stared at Rhys in surprise. 'This man continues to amaze me. Every day almost, I hear the most intriguing things about him. And all the while my respect and, yes, my admiration for him grows. I am afraid that if he manages to gain a strong enough following this coming summer, he may yet prove just as much a thorn in our new King's flesh as the Scots and the French.'

'That may well be so. Meanwhile, what are Bolingbroke's latest terms?'

Hotspur sighed and was silent for a moment. 'I'm afraid it is not what you want to hear, although an improvement on the previous set. The last time we spoke Henry was adamant that there would be no pardons and you would all pay the full penalty for treason against the Crown. After much urging from me he has now conceded pardons for you and twenty of your men, but he is determined that the remaining twenty be executed.'

'Never,' Rhys murmured quietly. 'We will all die here together as martyrs to the cause.'

'I was afraid you would say that. I am therefore instructed to tell you that, exceptionally, the King will agree to reduce the number to be killed from twenty to twelve.'

'Eight,' Rhys said with finality.

'I am sorry, Rhys, but the King assured me that twelve was his final word on the matter.'

'Then you can inform him that mine is eight.'

'You drive a hard bargain, Rhys, one which may well rebound on you, for Henry can be very stubborn.' But there was more than a hint of respect in Percy's voice. 'I will be able to pass on his reply to you within a couple of days, for the King is already on his way to Chester. He wants your unlucky twelve to be hanged, drawn and quartered in his presence before the assembled populace of Chester within the week.'

'Well, I regret to inform you but Bolingbroke will have a much longer wait while we all slowly die of hunger here in Conwy. Furthermore, he will not have his show for the good citizens of Chester as there will be no-one left alive to hang!'

'I wish you luck, Welshman. This is the last time we

two will parley in Conwy for I am called back to Chester to confer with the King and, regrettably, to endure all the horrors of the executions by his side.'

'With you gone, who will we be dealing with?' asked Rhys.

'Left to me, Rhys, it would be Massy, but knowing Henry I would not be surprised if he chooses the loathsome Fellows.'

'Then the young fool had better learn civility, or he may never see his King again,' Rhys growled.

Three days later, John Fellows arrived at the gatehouse seeking urgent talks with Rhys. Keen to know what King Henry's reaction had been to the latest parley with Hotspur, Rhys agreed to an immediate meeting. Even though the day was hot, Rhys offered no refreshments to the young man, whose demeanour was, if anything, even more superior and self-important than ever. Rhys sat in the Constable's chair behind the large desk and offered his visitor a seat.

'That will not be necessary,' Fellows responded, waving a hand airily. 'This meeting need only take a few minutes.'

Rhys raised his eyebrows but made no comment.

'The King,' Fellows continued, 'has instructed me to tell you that exceptionally, and in order to bring this situation to a speedy close, he has agreed to your suggestion that you should all be pardoned for your treacherous actions with the exception of eight of your followers. They will face the ultimate penalty for treason. Accordingly, the eight will be hanged, drawn and quartered publicly in Chester a week from today, in the presence of the King himself and the people of that city.'

'And if I agree, how do you intend to proceed with implementing the agreement?'

'That will be quite straightforward. At nine o'clock tomorrow morning you will send out the eight doomed men, unarmed and with their hands bound behind their backs. We will take them into custody, and the following morning we will send them under armed guard to Chester.'

Fellows paused and smiled sardonically. 'They will be placed in one of our large transport wagons so that they will be fresh and rested for the joys of execution in Chester.'

'You callous bastard,' Rhys's voice trembled with outrage. 'One day, soon, Master Fellows, you and I are going to meet somewhere without witnesses… and you will die… slowly.'

Fellows listened to the cold conviction in Rhys ap Tudur's voice and blanched. 'Y… you would not dare… I am the King's personal representative…'

'Oh, I would, Master Fellows… I would,' said Rhys quietly. 'In fact being the usurper Bolingbroke's representative makes you an even more attractive proposition.'

Rhys watched as the young man's mouth worked soundlessly, for the words would not come.

'Barbarian,' he spluttered eventually, and hurried out of the room as Rhys rose to his feet.

When he, in turn, left the room, the Welshman was smiling, but his eyes were cold as ice.

5

Apart from two sentries, Gwilym ap Tudur had mustered the entire company in the great banqueting hall an hour before supper. The high-ceilinged hall, which normally echoed to loud voices and laughter as the men assembled for their evening meal, was very quiet and the tension palpable. Word had sped rapidly around the castle that everyone, other than the sentries, was required in the great hall for an update on their situation following that morning's meeting with John Fellows. It was pretty evident that matters were rapidly heading towards a climax. They were also aware that they would not all be permitted to leave the castle without some of their number having to make the ultimate sacrifice. It was really a question of how many would have to face death to satisfy the vengeful English King.

With a creaking of hinges, the oak door behind the high table opened and Rhys ap Tudur entered, followed closely by his brother Gwilym, Gerwyn Dal and Meurig ap Siôn. All four sat at the table for a few moments before Rhys got to his feet to address the company.

'My brothers-in-arms, valiant and true, I salute

you.' The men seated at tables around the hall got up immediately and stood to attention. 'Thank you, now you can all sit down and relax. Today, my officers and I wish to salute you for your bravery, for your loyalty, and for your devotion to the cause which our Prince has begun in order to free all of Wales from the English. You all joined me in capturing this English stronghold on All Fools' Day. And, by the bones of our ancestors, what fools we made of them.'

His men roared their delight, banging tables and stamping on the floor.

'They are the laughing stock of all of Wales, all of England and even beyond these shores. By the same token, your fame, yes your fame, a small band of Welsh heroes, has spread far and wide. Not only have you wrested the castle from its garrison but you then managed to hold it against an army of twelve hundred for three months!'

Again roars of appreciation reverberated around the hall. Rhys raised his hand for silence. 'Unfortunately, in war there is never any gain without loss. We all knew when we came here that there would be a price to pay, because in taking the castle we were cutting ourselves off from our own people and, when the food ran out, we would be faced with some pretty stark choices. That day, my friends, has arrived. As you know we had three choices, none of which were appealing. One was to attempt a breakout (probably at night), but with the castle under siege by more than a thousand men, this would have been suicidal. Another would have been to stay here until we perished from hunger. That way, the English would regain control of the castle but we would all have died a dreadful death. The third choice, and I believe the best of a bad lot, was to negotiate terms of surrender with the King. When those negotiations started the King was in no mood to compromise. He wanted a full surrender and we would all die the death of traitors. Well, there was no question of us accepting that. He then came back with another offer. This time he would pardon me and five others of my choice and everyone else would be executed. After we had refused that, he offered to pardon me and half my force but the remaining half would die. I then asked Hotspur to help with negotiations. I am convinced that he did his best on our behalf. The problem, though, is that Henry is determined to put on a show in Chester by executing a number of us in public, as a warning to others that attacking English castles is not a good idea.'

Rhys paused as an angry muttering began around the tables. 'Hotspur came to me with terms which would allow everyone, bar twelve, to go free. I held out against that. And then came the final offer, which was to pardon and free everyone apart from eight of our number.'

There were angry shouts at this until Rhys held up his hand once more and the great hall gradually fell silent again.

'I honestly believe we now have the best terms we are likely to get. Any fewer than eight, and Henry's show in Chester would have looked pretty inadequate. It does mean that at least thirty-four of us will live to fight another day.'

There was a glum silence for a moment. A large man with wild ginger hair stood up. His deep bass boomed around the hall.

'That is one way of looking at it, I suppose. I would probably see it in that way too if I knew I had already been pardoned, and was safe anyway. Not such a great deal when it is possible that you could be one of the unlucky eight though, is it?'

Gwilym angrily rose to his feet, hand clenched on the hilt of his sword. 'Enough, Siôn Coch. That is no way to address your leader.'

Siôn Coch returned his stare without flinching. 'I mean no disrespect, Gwilym ap Tudur. I simply said the truth and that which all my comrades here think, but will not say.' The big man slowly subsided onto his chair still holding his head high.

Rhys motioned to Gwilym to resume his seat and straightened his back. 'My brothers, what Siôn said is, indeed, true. That is why I have decided that everyone's name, including mine, will be placed in the pot of chance later this evening when it is time to name the unfortunate eight.'

There was a shocked silence for a moment, then the company rose as one and Siôn Coch held up his hand. 'I salute you as a fair and courageous leader, Rhys ap Tudur, and I apologise for my earlier lack of faith.' The bass voice trembled slightly with emotion. 'If you and I survive this, I pledge to you, in front of everyone present, that I will give you loyal and unstinting service for the remainder of my days, and that I will offer my life for yours if ever that situation should arise.'

There was loud cheering for several minutes until Rhys called them again to order, before thanking Siôn Coch and all the company for their support and announcing that dinner would be served. Knowing that they would all be leaving the castle in the morning, Rhys had instructed the kitchen staff to provide the best fare possible from their depleted food stocks. The meal was much better than any they had eaten for weeks but the atmosphere was unnaturally muted. Everyone was acutely aware that they would soon be involved in the process of determining who the eight condemned men would be.

Finally, after the servants had cleared away the dishes and all the hall's doors were closed once more, Rhys stood up and every man fell silent. He looked drawn and tired as he cleared his throat.

'Well, my friends, we are now faced with the task we have all been dreading. Yet while it is a totally distasteful one, it is staring us all in the face and has to be done. I confess I could think of no method of doing this which would be fair to one and all. With your agreement, I intend to leave it to fate, or chance, call it what you will, to decide. There is one among us, an Englishman no less, who will not be directly involved in the procedure, so I have asked him to conduct it. I speak of Tom Easton who was forced to take part in the act of taking the castle. We, of course, have turned him into a Welsh-speaking Englishman who, I feel sure you will agree, has served us well in our enterprise.'

There was a quiet murmur of agreement which pleased Rhys for he had grown to like the carpenter. His courtship of Gwen, the serving maid, had made him the butt of much leg-pulling, which he had taken in good part. Thanks to Gwen's Welsh lessons, Tom had become fluent enough to do some teasing of his own in Welsh, much to everyone's amusement.

'Tom, would you bring the pail with wooden pegs in to the end of the top table please?'

Turning back to the company, he explained what each man would need to do.

'In a moment we will form a line, table by table, one behind the other. The four of us at top table will line up behind table two, in other words right in your midst. Each man in turn will walk forward to the pail, supervised by Tom Easton, place his right hand inside it and draw out one wooden peg. You are to look away from the pail as you reach for the peg. You will then walk back to your place at table and stand still until everyone has done the same. During this wait you will keep the peg in your hand, at your side, without looking at it. Anyone seen examining the peg before being told to do so will be named a condemned man, whatever the peg reveals. Is that clear? No questions? Good. Table one, stand and make your way forward.'

The men's faces expressed a myriad of emotions as they slowly trooped forward. Some tried to present a confident grin, others looked at the ground to try to hide their feelings, while a few looked truly terrified – too frightened to care who else knew how they felt. At length, every man in the room had returned to his former position, wooden peg in hand.

'We will now sit and examine the pegs.'

There was a hurried scraping of chair legs as everyone sat down.

'If you look closely some of you will see a cross carved on the side of the peg. Others will have unmarked pegs.

I have to tell you that there are only eight pegs with a cross marked on them. I need say no more.'

For a moment there was silence. Then, there was frenzied pandemonium as friends with unmarked pegs shouted at each other and clasped each other with joy and relief, while a minority sat stonily, staring at their pegs in horrified disbelief.

After several minutes Rhys got to his feet once more. He looked pale and shaken. Everyone looked up and noticed the change in him, and suddenly the hall was silent.

He cleared his throat and swallowed. When he spoke his voice was unusually hoarse.

'Will the eight who drew a peg marked with a cross – stand?' There was a murmur of sympathy from the relieved, lucky ones as the eight rose to their feet. One of them had been seated at the top table. It was Gwilym ap Tudur.

Later, the two brothers stood on the battlements looking towards their native Anglesey, oblivious to the steady drizzle which had swept in from the sea on a westerly breeze some hours earlier. The island was not visible in the darkness and the rain, but both seemed to draw comfort from the knowledge that it was only a few short miles away across the water. They stood there for a long time in silence, each lost in his own thoughts. Gwilym's sudden and unexpected inclusion as one of the doomed eight, facing the cruellest of executions, had temporarily numbed their faculties, making both incapable of coherent thought. Finally, as if by telepathic contact, they roused themselves, turned and walked across to the north tower and, with no exchange of words, made their way to their sleeping quarters. Outside the door to Rhys's chamber, he turned and said gruffly, 'You had better come in for a while. We have a lot of talking – and thinking, to do.'

Gwilym went over to a settle by the fireplace. There was no fire in the grate and he shivered as he sat down, even though it was summer. He watched his elder brother pouring some of the Constable's best wine from a pitcher on his table into two goblets. Rhys's face looked old and worn in the yellow light of the tallow candles. He handed Gwilym one of the goblets and sat in a high-backed chair opposite the settle.

'I don't see what there is to talk or think about, Rhys,' Gwilym sighed. 'The situation is pretty cut and dried it seems to me. Tomorrow, I will be handed over to the English to be taken to Chester. In a couple of days' time I will be butchered there in front of the King and hundreds of jeering commoners.'

'There are other options to consider…'

'Such as?'

'Such as letting me take your place, little brother. After all, you would not be in this position but for me.'

'Oh come on, Rhys. You know I would never knowingly allow you to sacrifice yourself for me. Would you let me sully my name, and the name of our family, in front of our comrades and the whole of Wales? No, do not insult me brother.'

'Gwilym, you know very well that it is not my intention to insult you. I have always done my best to protect you and the offer is just my clumsy way of suggesting a means of protecting you from this horror.'

Gwilym smiled for the first time. 'That I know, and though I have never before thanked you for everything you have done for me since childhood, I am glad of the chance to do so now, for you are the best elder brother any man could ever hope for.'

Rhys said nothing but stared hard at the floor. When he got up to fetch them more wine the candlelight revealed tears in his eyes. Gwilym stared at him in astonishment, for it was a sight he could not remember ever having seen before.

Before either could say any more, they heard the sound of footsteps in the corridor outside. The footsteps stopped, and there was a sharp knock on the door.

'Come,' Rhys called.

Meurig ap Siôn swung the door open and hurried in, accompanied by a cold-looking Tom Easter, his clothes soaking wet and exceedingly smelly.

'I hope you don't mind our interruption at this late hour but Tom has news, and we also have some ideas which may interest you. Ah Gwilym, you are here already. Good. I'm sure that what we have to say will be of particular interest to you.'

'Well, whatever it is, it will have to wait till poor Tom has changed into some dry clothes,' said Rhys firmly. 'Gwilym, he is almost as tall as you, take him to your chamber and lend him some dry clothing.'

Rhys and Meurig sat at the table for a while sipping wine, content to wait for the others to return before beginning to discuss the news. Tom and Gwilym were soon back. Tom looked distinctly more comfortable and relaxed in borrowed jerkin and braies. They, too, took seats at the table and Meurig cleared his throat, eager to begin.

'You may wish to know that Tom has been on a visit to town this evening.' The archers' leader grinned broadly as he saw the startled expressions on the brothers' faces. 'Now Rhys, before you start blaming me for permitting him to go, let me assure you that I had no idea of his intentions until he returned to the castle, a short while ago.'

'Have you lost your mind, Tom?' asked Rhys severely.

'How on earth did you manage to get out, and back again, without being seen? Come to think of it, why would you come back anyway, seeing as we are all leaving in the morning?'

Thomas looked at each in turn and smiled before answering.

'Since you kidnapped me I've been doing a lot of thinking. Although you forced me to join you in taking the castle, you have always treated me with respect. I have listened to the men describe how you and your families are treated by my countrymen, having no rights in English law, being heavily taxed and generally looked down upon as inferiors in your own country. All this is obviously wrong and, as an Englishman, I cannot defend such practices. In fact, I know your cause is just. I am no soldier, nor do I have much understanding of politics, but I really do want to help and I believe there are many ways in which I can help you. For a start, having an English accent could be of help from time to time. It certainly was tonight.' He grinned mysteriously.

'Your point is well made,' Rhys acknowledged. 'Tell us what happened tonight. We are all bursting to know.'

'This afternoon I had an idea,' Thomas continued. 'Since this is the last night of a long siege and we've agreed to surrender the castle, I thought the English soldiers would be overjoyed and in a mood to celebrate. The chances were that their sentries would be less vigilant, with their thoughts more on cursing their luck at being on duty while their fellows were enjoying food, ale and, of course, women. They would probably reason that nobody would break out of the castle because the majority, who have been offered the King's pardon, will want to ensure that the condemned eight are safely under lock and key.'

'That, I would say, was a brave if foolhardy assumption,' Gwilym murmured, but there was a new respect in his eyes as he stared at the carpenter.

Tom laughed. 'Be that as it may, it was a good guess.'

He described how he had persuaded a guard to open the small pedestrian door facing onto the drawbridge, waiting for the moon to disappear behind a cloud before easing himself out into the shadows. He had then slipped quietly into the stinking waters of the moat and, half-swimming, half-wading, had slowly made his way to the other side, keeping himself in the intense darkness of the drawbridge's superstructure, so as not to be seen by the two sentries on the town side. Having reached a position directly beneath the planking where the sentries stood, it was easy to listen to their conversation. At first he had thought he was wasting his time for, as he had guessed, the two were thoroughly fed up with being on duty when the majority of their colleagues were enjoying themselves in the makeshift hostelries which had sprung up in the town in the past few months to provide the large military force with off-duty revelry.

He was debating whether to move upstream and make his way into the town when the sentries' chat moved on to some interesting disclosures. Hotspur had left for Chester, taking his personal retinue of three hundred with him. A force of more than two hundred rebels had laid siege to Caernarfon castle in the name of Glendower some days ago and, that very morning, Massy had left for Caernarfon with a detachment of three hundred of the most experienced campaigners available. His objective was to force the Welsh to raise the siege, or gain a decisive victory should they decide to stand their ground and fight. The remaining force of four hundred and fifty in Conwy was under the direct military control of the most experienced officer available, a certain Guy Falconer. However, he was answerable in all things other than direct military engagement, to John Fellows. The King had decreed that until the rebellion was quashed, Conwy castle would be constantly garrisoned by no less than two hundred men. So, when the eight condemned Welshmen were sent to Chester, their armed guard would consist of the other two hundred and fifty men. Thomas paused while his avid listeners waited impatiently for more.

'Finally,' he said conspiratorially, 'Captain Guy Falconer is to stay here to command the garrison, so the force guarding the prisoners on the journey to Chester will be led by John Fellows.'

All the others gasped in disbelief.

'But that is incredible,' protested Meurig ap Siôn. 'How could anyone entrust that task to a young idiot like Fellows, who has probably never held sword in hand in his life.'

'The sentries were agreed on that as well,' said Tom. 'I think that decision was taken by the young fool himself. After all, there is no-one here to curb him now. They thought Fellows was banking on the fact that if Glyndŵr's cause is as poorly supported as the King believes, then the besiegers of Caernarfon probably represent his entire strength. So, having retaken Conwy castle, the English will have regained their reputation as an unbeatable foe. Add to that the fact that eight of the heroes who took Conwy castle are now on their way to the gallows will be enough to cow any would-be rebels thinking of joining Glyndŵr.'

'For someone who claims not to be a soldier, and who has no understanding of politics, your reasoning is very impressive Tom,' said Rhys with a grin. 'Your initiative tonight has been as successful as it was unexpected, and I'm sure the others will agree with me that the information you have uncovered is, and will be, of tremendous value to us in the coming days. Well done.'

There was a chorus of acclaim from the others, with Gwilym delivering several hearty claps on the back which resulted in Thomas succumbing to a fit of coughing.

'One more thing, Tom. Did they say when, exactly, this great leader of men will begin the journey to Chester?' Rhys's voice sounded excited and animated at the thought that there might yet be some way of regaining the initiative and saving his men from a barbaric death in Chester.

'Yes, they intend starting in the early morning, the day after tomorrow. They will transport the prisoners tied up in one of their long transport wagons, which are normally drawn by four oxen. This is bound to slow them down. Yet, by starting at dawn, they still hope to reach Chester in maybe two days… or certainly in three.'

'Gentlemen, I think it time we were in our beds,' said Rhys decisively. 'Tomorrow will be a long and difficult one for us all in different ways. I think it important that we make no mention of the information, so bravely discovered by Tom tonight, to anyone else. We don't want the other condemned men to know that there is a slim hope of survival, in case they behave in a manner which could alert the enemy to potential trouble. There is nothing to be gained by informing the others, either, until we get well away from Conwy. The fewer who know a secret, the more secure the secret. Do you agree?'

The other three nodded vigorously.

'Gwilym, you will join the other seven early in the morning. You will have to submit to the indignity of having your hands tied behind you just like the others and remember… tell them nothing of tonight's events.'

'Don't worry about me – I know how to keep my mouth shut, and I shall be alert to any move you may make to release us, whenever that happens.' With that he grabbed Rhys's shoulders and shook him roughly before leaving the chamber without another word.

'Tomorrow, as soon as we get some miles between us and this place, we will hold a meeting to which Gerwyn Dal will also be invited,' said Rhys briskly. 'We will share the information with Gerwyn, then try to work out an effective strategy to gain the release of Gwilym and the others. We will need Owain's help to do it, so we must find out how to make contact with him, as soon as possible. Now, away to your beds. Let's try and get some rest. God knows, we shall have more than enough on our hands come morning.'

6

A T NINE O'CLOCK the following morning the great doors of Conwy castle creaked and groaned as the little-used hinges took the strain, and opened slowly. Standing at the head of the Welsh column drawn up in the castle courtyard in ranks, four abreast, Gerwyn Dal's first view was across the drawbridge where a large force of English soldiers stood waiting. The danger of the situation was not lost on the seasoned campaigner. If the English King had broken his word and given his men orders to attack as soon as the small band left the castle, the Welsh would not stand a chance. A man in full battle armour strode across the drawbridge at the head of two rows of pikemen who took up positions on either side, leaving a passage down the middle.

Rhys ap Tudur studied the officer closely. This was Captain Guy Falconer, obviously an experienced soldier, confident and capable. Rhys felt a grudging respect for the man.

'In the name of the King,' Falconer called out, 'I order you to send forth the eight condemned men with hands tied behind their backs.'

'We honour our agreement, Captain. I hereby hand

over the eight men into your custody. I trust they will be treated honourably while in your care.'

'You are in no position to claim any privileges for them, Welshman. However, the King will not want them half-dead when they get to Chester, so they will be travelling under royal protection,' Falconer responded stiffly.

'Thank you, Captain.'

Rhys turned and nodded to Meurig ap Siôn who led the line of eight men, with their hands tied behind their backs, as far as the castle entrance. Then they continued down the passageway between the two rows of pikemen who closed in behind them, forming a protective wedge of steel around the prisoners. As they reached the end of the drawbridge and disappeared from view, they were subjected to shouted insults and jeers from the townsfolk and some of the off-duty soldiers.

The departed pikemen were now replaced by two double rows of more pikemen. Rhys smiled a mirthless smile. Falconer was taking no chances with his safety, or that of his thirty-two men, as they left the castle.

In a narrow second-floor window of the north tower, Thomas Easton and Gwen observed the scene, having a clear view of the castle entrance and the drawbridge beyond. It had been agreed with Rhys that Thomas would leave that evening with a group of castle servants, who would be free for the first time in three months to go out for a night on the town. After getting clear of the town, he was to follow Rhys Ddu's depleted Welsh force into the woods and hills to the south of Conwy, hopefully reaching their overnight camp in the tiny hamlet of Gelli Hir before dawn. The couple watched the departure of their friends with heavy hearts, aware that in a few short hours they, too, would be parted for the first time since becoming lovers, not knowing when or where they would be together again.

As the Welsh band, with their protective rows of pikemen, reached the end of the drawbridge, there was a surge in the crowd as some of the townsmen angrily attempted to reach them. The pikemen held firm though, and shouted warnings to the crowd that if they tried to attack again the pikes would be used to deadly effect, in the King's name. There was no more jostling but the Welshmen had to endure shouted insults and a hail of rotten vegetables and eggs until, at last, they were allowed out of the walled town's gates.

Back in the north tower of Conwy castle Tom and Gwen sighed with relief, having witnessed their friends' safe, if noisy, departure. Tom cupped Gwen's face in his hands and gazed into her eyes, disturbed by the love, the longing and the sadness in them. Gently he laid her down onto a pile of sweet-smelling hay. She clung to him hungrily as he kissed her on the mouth with mounting passion. Then, with a groan of pleasure and pent-up need, he covered her with his body.

Rhys, meanwhile, kept his men moving at a punishing pace. Covered in muck but feeling bullish in the fresh summer air, they sang their marching song as they strode south, finally reaching the welcome protection of the trees. As soon as they entered the woods Gerwyn Dal called a short break. Marching would be impossible in the undergrowth so he set them to walk in single file along the only clear way ahead – a narrow, uneven and winding path.

As a safety precaution, he sent two archers on ahead as scouts with orders to stay hidden and return immediately to report the sighting of anyone, friend or foe. Although it was a hot day they travelled for the most part under the canopy of deciduous woodland in full summer leaf, out of the glare of the sun. They made good time until, in the early afternoon, they came to a small, fast-moving stream. Rhys called a halt in a secluded clearing, so that the men could slake their thirst and rest. Most of them flung off their clothes and washed themselves and their clothing in the cool, clear water of the stream before lying down in the shade to rest their aching limbs. It was a real pleasure to lie down on grass after three months in a stone castle, and to tramp through woods redolent with the distinctive aroma of wild garlic. They thought of their comrades destined for the most bestial of executions in Chester in the next few days, a fate too ghastly to contemplate. It still came as a shock to realise how it could very easily have been any one of them in the condemned party.

Rhys was about to call the men back to their stations when he was startled by one of the perimeter guards shouting a challenge. Everyone else heard it as well and there was a flurry of movement as they all scurried to retrieve their weapons to face whatever danger might present itself. They heard a voice answering the guard's challenge in measured tones and seconds later the guard appeared, accompanied by a young man with wild hair, his clothing mostly of animal skins, wearing a well-worn leather belt with a short sword in a battered leather scabbard. He carried a round shield on his back coloured a drab green, but with strange magical symbols etched in black.

'This is Rhys Gethin, my lord,' the guard announced. 'He claims to bear a message for you from Prince Owain ap Gruffudd Fychan.'

'Henffych.' Rhys ap Tudur gave the traditional polite greeting, at the same time studying the young man closely. He was of medium height and build with a wiry frame. His clothing and dark restless eyes revealed his wild hill man heritage but his voice, when he spoke, hinted at an intelligence and a perceptiveness which belied his appearance.

'Rhys ap Tudur?' He accepted Rhys's nod and continued,' I bring you greetings from your cousin, Owain. He wants you to know that he and a force of eighty archers and forty men-at-arms are within a few miles of Gelli Hir and if you get there by nightfall you can, between you, decide what action to take to try and save your eight comrades held as prisoners by the English. Tomorrow, we can all march to join a much larger force which is already preparing a warm welcome for the English detachment escorting your companions to Chester.'

Rhys Gethin smiled before adding, 'He also asked me to pass on his warm congratulations to you for capturing and holding Conwy castle for so long. I would like to add my own congratulations as well. Your action came at exactly the right time, when many of our followers were beginning to lose heart. Now, thanks to you and your men, the whole of Wales is filled with new hope. Every day we receive envoys from different parts of the country, pledging support.'

At these words, Rhys ap Tudur's men, who had listened in silence to Gethin's words, broke into a loud cheer, visibly filled with pride.

'There you are my friend. You can see the spirit of the men I lead.' He placed his arm around Rhys Gethin's shoulder. 'We have roughly two hours of walking ahead of us. Let us walk together, for I have much to ask you.

I am anxious to know of Owain's activities since we took the castle and you, probably, have questions for me.'

As they led the rest down the rough footpath, Rhys ap Tudur was full of curiosity about his young companion. It was said that Rhys Gethin was pretty useful with the sword and with his fists. He was known to prefer living among his own hill folk and hated being confined within castle walls and sleeping in a proper bed. It was also rumoured that he was an illegitimate son of Owain Glyndŵr…

'I suppose you must be wondering why Owain decided to lay siege to Caernarfon castle with a meagre two hundred men, now that you know he could have used a far bigger force,' said Rhys Gethin, as they walked purposefully towards Gelli Hir.

'There can only be one answer to that now that I know, as you say, that he had more resources available.'

'And that is?' Rhys Gethin enquired quizzically.

'What you must realise, young Rhys, is that you are speaking to someone who is not exactly new to warfare and military tactics,' his namesake grinned. 'Owain, masterly general that he is, would have been aware that there must be various pressures on us to give up Conwy castle by now, not least being a diminishing supply of food. He could not know how we planned to get out of Conwy with minimum casualties, but it did strike him that a diversion, such as a less than impressive siege of another castle in the area, would tempt Bolingbroke to send several hundred crack soldiers from the large contingent in Conwy, to attack that besieging force. The fewer English soldiers left in Conwy, the better would be our chances to escape from the castle. The siege of Caernarfon castle was simply a diversion which would help us free ourselves from Conwy.'

'I see that I am speaking to a wise professional. Forgive me for presuming that you might not have been.'

Rhys ap Tudur turned to look at his young companion, and saw that his face was red with embarrassment. He laughed aloud and young Gethin, suddenly seeing the funny side of the situation, laughed too, relieved that the older man had taken it all in good part.

7

T HE MIDDAY SUN beat down mercilessly on the sweating prisoners, each stripped to the waist and chained to an iron bar attached to the inner sides of the long wagon. Several groaned as the wagon, drawn by four oxen, clattered over some uneven stones on the rough coastal path, shaking them severely for the hundredth time since leaving Conwy that morning. In places the road was no wider than a footpath and the wagon's wheels slammed into ruts and unforgiving boulders with painful regularity. The eight sat facing inwards, four on each side, and despite sweating profusely they could feel the sun burning the tender flesh of their shoulders and backs.

The summer heat and the rough track were not all they had to endure. Alfred, the foul-mouthed wagon driver and their lumbering guard, Harold, had decided that while the prisoners were not to be physically harmed, on the King's orders, it would be an entertaining diversion to subject them to some mental torture, to pass the time. Gruesome tales of people being hanged, drawn and quartered had been the main subject of a conversation conducted in loud voices, so that the chained men would hear every word. These executions were portrayed in gory detail and at one stage the youngest of the prisoners, a sixteen-year-old lad called Esmor, had vomited. He had been roundly cursed by Harold and told he would have to clean up the mess before being given any food or rest at the next stop.

''Ere 'Arold, now I do believe that the first man to be butchered in this way was a Welshman, back in the days of the first King Edward.'

''Twas in Shrewsbury, my home town, an' all.'

'You don't say. 'Ow long ago would that be, Alfie?' Harold casually wiped his nose before drying his hand on his sleeve.

'Oh, got to be a 'undred year ago, maybe more…' A broad smile crossed Alfred's face as he raised his voice a little. 'Yeah, he were the son of some Welsh prince… er… prince of Gweenid, I think. Fancied himself as a bit of a rebel, like.'

'Don't suppose 'e 'ad much idea what was comin' like, him bein' the first, an' all,' said Harold profoundly.

'Well, 'e 'ad a bit of a surprise then, didn' 'e?' Alfred cackled gleefully. 'The knife 'appened to be a bit on the blunt side…' Here the storyteller paused and glanced around at his captive audience.

'First of all they 'anged 'im, but not long enough to kill 'im, see. Then they cut 'im down and stripped 'im and threw a bucket of water over 'im, to wake 'im up. Ah dear, took a long time to cut off 'is privates, like, the knife bein' blunt d'ye see. Hah! They say he screamed so loud they could 'ear 'im in bleedin' Gweenid. He was close to faintin' after tha', but two 'eld 'im while the 'angman drove the knife into 'is groin and opened him up to the chest, like guttin' a fish. Can you imagine the 'orror in 'is eyes as all those warm, slippery guts spilled out of 'im onto the floor like... 'orrible it were... No more bein' a rebel, eh?'

The driver and guard laughed heartily. Alfred turned to look at the ashen faces, noting with satisfaction the effect of his colourful description on the prisoners.

As he was turning away, one of them cleared his throat and said quietly, 'I make you this promise, Alfred. If, through some stroke of luck, I ever get the chance to pay you back for this morning's entertainment, be it in this world or the next, it will be exactly as you have just described, and my knife will be a very blunt one...'

Alfred opened his mouth to bluster but froze as he saw the cold certainty of the promise in the eyes of Gwilym ap Tudur.

At the head of the column John Fellows, accompanied by Roderick Stone, an experienced sergeant-at-arms, rode a large black destrier, cutting a comical figure in unfamiliar, ill-fitting armour and a long sword which was obviously much too heavy for a man of his physique. Roderick Stone bore an appearance of thinly hidden embarrassment to be riding alongside such a parody of a commanding officer. However, Stone was an experienced professional soldier and he comforted himself that this journey to Chester would be the first and, in all probability, the last time that John Fellows would be given a military command of any kind. Indeed, if Bolingbroke should happen to witness their entry into the city, Stone felt sure that Fellows would be in for a verbal lashing for having assumed command at all. He had done his best to suggest the most effective deployment of their force for the journey, but he had the uneasy feeling that Fellows might well ignore his suggestions if they came under any kind of pressure. So far they had had a hot, exhausting and exceedingly boring journey along the north Wales coast. He was on the point of suggesting a pause to rest awhile when one of the three scouts they had sent ahead came galloping back to them.

'My lord,' the man was breathless and his horse was blowing heavily. 'About two miles down the road we found a traveller, an Englishman, badly beaten and lying by the roadside. He said that earlier this morning he stumbled upon a large force of armed Welshmen, resting on a grassy spot either side of the path. They seized him, thinking he was one of our scouts.

'They questioned the man, whose name is Thomas, as they believed he was one of our scouts. When he could not provide details of our force, and our whereabouts, they tried to beat the information out of him. They eventually gave up, tied him and took him with them, boasting that they knew we were following the coastal route, and that they would prepare a warm welcome for us, long before we reached Chester. Later, he managed to escape. They pursued him but he hid among reeds in an area of marshland. They seemed in a hurry to get to their planned ambush point, so they left when they failed to find him.'

'Did he have any idea of how big a force we are facing?' Roderick Stone asked thoughtfully.

'I asked him that,' said the scout. 'He thought there were at least a couple of hundred, and possibly a lot more. He also suggested that we travel inland a few miles, then follow an inland route eastwards for fifteen miles or so before rejoining the easier coastal path for the last leg of the journey to Chester. That would almost certainly take us past the Welsh ambush, for they would not relish venturing much closer to Chester knowing that the King is encamped there with an army of several thousand.'

'That sounds a very sensible suggestion,' said Commander John Fellows, speaking for the first time. 'Our orders are clear. Our duty is to journey to Chester to join the King's forces and to deliver the eight rebels to their execution.'

'But my lord, we have a chance here of gaining much respect from the King by defeating a fairly large band of Glendower's men and so driving another nail into the coffin of this paltry rebellion. Now that we know they are expecting us we have an advantage, for they will still believe we are unaware of their presence. We can make plans to surprise them and show them that they can't take on a trained English army.'

Some of the men who were within earshot made exclamations of support for Stone's view. This seemed to annoy Fellows for he turned on his officer…

'Enough. There are too many doubts attached to that argument, Stone. Firstly, we do not know the enemy's exact strength. We have two hundred and forty men. They may have twice that number. At worst, we could be defeated and lose both the prisoners and the tax revenues we are transporting. What do you think the King would think of us then? Furthermore, even if we did defeat them, a battle might allow opportunities for the prisoners to escape. Reporting a victory over the Welsh at the expense of losing the prisoners he wants to make an example of would hardly endear us to his Majesty.'

'But, sir, can we wait at least until we reach this Thomas and question him ourselves? That would…'

'No,' Fellows barked. 'As commander here I have made my decision. We will stick to our orders and get the prisoners safely to the King. Nothing must interfere with that, and certainly not an unnecessary confrontation with some Welsh ruffians. Let that be the end of the matter.'

'Yes, sir.' Roderick Stone gritted his teeth, resisting the urge to defy the young popinjay and risk being charged with insubordination. Instead, he crisply dismissed the scout and instructed the junior officers to get the men ready to continue down the path to where the injured Englishman was being tended by the other two scouts.

They found the man being helped to his feet by the two outriders in a small clearing where the path broadened out a little. Fellows dismounted immediately and hurried over to question the man, closely followed by Stone.

'Well, my man, I want you to tell me exactly what happened to you. Also, I want to know who you are, where you come from, where your home is and why you were on this road when the Welsh villains caught you. I need not remind you that if you tell me anything other than the truth, your fate will be death by hanging.'

Tom swallowed and swayed slightly, still groggy from his ordeal.

'May I suggest, sire, that we allow the poor fellow to

sit on this rock while we interrogate him,' said Stone quietly.

'Very well. Sit him down for he is still affected by his mishap,' Fellows responded, displaying an uncharacteristic streak of compassion.

Tom sat on the rock and began his tale while his two interrogators examined the livid bruises and nasty cuts to face and body, which bore witness to a severe beating.

'My name is Thomas Easton. My home was in Conwy until the day when the accursed Welshmen tricked their way into the castle and burnt the town.'

'You do not sound like a common peasant, Tom,' Fellows interjected. 'As a burgher of Conwy I reckon you were an artisan of some kind.'

'My lord, I was a carpenter and did a lot of work for Constable Massy at the castle. I moved there some four years ago after my wife and children died of the plague, in Chester. Before that, I was employed in the King's army as a carpenter, bowyer and fletcher.'

'Where had you been before you were attacked, and what was your destination?' asked Roderick Stone.

'After the burning of Conwy I returned to my old mother's home in Chester for I was homeless, with little hope of immediate work in Conwy. I was on my way back to Conwy though when I was attacked, for everyone in Chester had heard, and rejoiced, at the news that Conwy castle was now back in the hands of the King. With the borough being rebuilt and once more under English control, there is hope of much profitable work for a good carpenter.'

Fellows and Stone looked at each other and nodded in unspoken agreement.

'There is no doubting that you have had a severe beating and you are obviously an industrious and honest Englishman, Thomas Easton. You are a good worker and a loyal subject to your King. Now tell me, what makes you think that for us to cut inland will be any safer than marching on along the coast to meet this Welsh rabble?' Fellows eyed him keenly.

'Oh my lord, the worst thing you can do is underestimate this Welsh force. As I say, they number at least two hundred and maybe as many as four hundred men. From their equipment, general confidence and deployment, I believe the majority of them are seasoned, professional soldiers who have probably seen service in the late King Richard's armies. For a Welsh company, they seemed well equipped. They are mostly longbow men, many of them mounted on those small but nimble mountain ponies, and you know the reputation Welsh archers have gained for themselves. They also have pikemen and infantry, mostly armed with swords and shields but with some wielding battleaxes. Even more importantly, although

I did not see him, there is little doubt that they are led by Owen Glendower himself. They are certainly carrying the royal standard of the princely House of Gweened – four lions rampant in red and gold. That standard can only be raised when the native Prince of Wales is present. I also heard say that they were carrying Glendower's personal war banner. This has mystical significance for the Welsh since the original was the banner of Uther Pendragon, the greatest of all the old British war leaders, centuries ago. It depicts a fierce golden dragon on a white background.'

Thomas paused before lowering his voice to a whisper. 'There is also a firm belief among them that Glendower has magical powers. Apparently, he can influence the heavenly bodies to induce storms, thunder and lightning and heavy rainfall. He professes to be a Christian, but it is known that in his youth he dabbled in the beliefs of the hill people who still secretly practise the ancient religion of the Druids.'

'Oh dear, come, come Tom,' Fellows laughed lightly. 'Do not get carried away by the wild fantasies of the ignorant. There are more tales told about this man than common sense can allow. We will be hearing next that he can walk on water.' Fellows turned to the others within earshot to see the amusement his words would have raised. There was a polite guffaw or two but none that was very convincing.

'Now, I want you all to listen to me,' he said tightly, disappointed by their reaction. 'I want no more talk of Glendower, the magician. To me he is no Druid but an ordinary man… a very… ordinary… Welshman, who needs to be taught some lessons. However, today is not the day for such actions. Our priority is to escort our eight Welsh prisoners safely to Chester. King Henry will soon be teaching the people of this area lessons they will never forget, with an army of many thousands, then Glendower and his fancy golden dragon will perish and order will be restored. But what of the route you were suggesting Master Thomas, to avoid the Welsh magician?'

'I have to confess, my lord, that I have no personal experience of this alternative route. But I remember speaking to a King's messenger years ago, who was similarly warned to avoid the next stretch of the coastal road to Chester. He claimed that if you walk six miles or so inland from here – there is a well-used trail leading inland just down the path from here – you will come to a wide, slow-moving stream or small river. I do not know what it is called. All you need do is turn eastward along the bank of that stream. The whole area, as you can imagine, is heavily wooded but there is a well-worn tract of open land along the banks of the stream for almost the whole journey. You will eventually reach a narrow valley where the stream becomes a ribbon-like, fast-moving streamlet. The stony ground of this valley may cause some difficulties for your wagons, but it is only a couple of miles long. Soon you will be back on the coastal road, some miles west of the borough of Flint. From there it is only a short journey to Chester.'

It did not take long for the broad details of the situation to filter through the ranks to the wagons. Initially, the prisoners were elated to learn that their compatriots were planning to ambush their English guards. Their spirits soon turned to despair as they heard how the column was planning to switch routes, travelling inland to avoid the Welsh ambush. Gwilym Tudur was the only one who maintained an apparent indifference to this last piece of news.

Fellows ordered that Tom Easton be allowed to lie down in one of the wagons, for he was still too groggy to walk any distance. Since the first wagon was loaded with chests of coins representing the King's tax revenue collected over the past three months from north-west Wales, and the two supply wagons were fully loaded, the only area where Tom could lie down was in the prisoners' wagon. Harold and Alfred laid some blankets on the floor of the wagon between the two rows of prisoners and Gwilym only had time for a quick, whispered, 'Don't let on you know him!' in Welsh, before Tom was helped into their midst. Several startled gasps were quickly stifled. The guard and driver were too intent on making the newcomer as comfortable as they could to notice the reaction.

'Sorry we 'ave to put you in with this scum, mister, but there is nowhere else, d'you see?' Harold apologised.

'Yeah,' echoed Alfred. 'And you'll 'ave to get used to them natterin' in that barbaric language. But not to worry, eh? You'll get yer own back tomorrow, like, when you get to see their guts bein' ripped out of 'em, eh?' Alfred chortled.

Tom twisted around so that he could look directly at Gwilym and made an unlocking motion with his hand. Gwilym understood and pointed to the heavy bunch of keys hanging from Harold's belt. Tom nodded and returned to a more relaxed position. There was quiet among the prisoners as the wagons continued on their way. The hooves of the horses and oxen were muffled by the short but lush grass along its bank and, eighty yards to their left, birds sang their praises to the summer god in the leafy greenery of the woods. A more tranquil setting was difficult to imagine.

At the head of the column, John Fellows and Roderick Stone rode side by side in a more sullen silence. Since their disagreement over whether to meet the Welsh ambush head-on or follow the alternative inland route to avoid it, the two had dropped all pretence at hiding their mutual dislike of each other. After another hour or so the stream had narrowed considerably, the flow was much quicker and they both realised that they were close to the narrow valley described by Tom.

'Why are you wearing such a worried frown, Stone?' Fellows asked suddenly.

'Here we are, travelling in quiet, safe countryside, our ability to deliver the prisoners and the tax revenues which the King so badly needs to pay his army now guaranteed, and you look as if you are expecting to be ambushed at any moment. For goodness sake smile, man, and think of how you can best spend the handsome bonus which will be yours tomorrow.' He turned to face the officer and bridled at the contemptuous stare which Stone made no attempt to hide.

'I realise there is no chance of convincing you of the potential threat we are about to face, but it is my duty to point it out to you.' Stone paused for a moment. 'No, don't interrupt. I am the man with the military experience here and I have a bad feeling... call it a foreboding if you like. It is my belief that the valley up ahead would be an ideal location to attack the column. It is, apparently, rocky and narrow. An excellent position to catch us when we may well be moving with difficulty, probably in single file, while the men at the rear have all sorts of problems getting the wagons through.'

'You are, indeed, the experienced military man, Roderick, and I do not deny that your assessment of the valley is correct. But you forget one thing. There will be nobody there to attack us because we have outwitted them. Was it not a true Englishman, beaten by those Welsh barbarians, who told us how to escape their clutches?'

'That is true enough. How do we know, though, that we were not seen changing course by one of Glendower's sympathisers? How do we know that he did not leave one or more scouts behind to see what we would do if, and when, we found Tom Easton? Have you thought about this at all?' Stone finished, his voice rising angrily.

'That will do, Stone,' snapped Fellows, conscious of a sudden nausea in the pit of his stomach as he realised that his safe haven might not be so safe after all. 'I… I… do not believe a word of it. We dispatched several of our men around that whole area when we questioned Easton, and all came back to report that they had seen no-one, friend or foe. No, I forbid any more such talk, or we will make the men nervous.'

With that, Fellows picked up the pace to distance himself from the taciturn veteran. Nevertheless, his calm conviction that they were safe from attack had been demolished. He swore at Stone under his breath and started to look around warily at his surroundings as he rode.

A little later they came around a bend in the stream

and saw, some three hundred yards in front of them, the entrance into the narrow valley. The grassy bank was now replaced by a gently rising, stony hillside, thirty yards wide and barren until the final approach to the valley entrance where some low brush and dusty bushes grew. The entrance itself was guarded on either side by tall crags.

Stone raised his hand and halted the column. Fellows, riding a few yards ahead turned his mount and approached Stone with a scowl on his face.

'Sire, I thought we should pause and examine this place before we proceed into the valley.'

Fellows, with his back to the valley, was on the point of chiding the man for his timidity when he saw the obstinate set of Stone's face change rapidly to a look of sheer incredulity. He spun his horse around as Stone shouted, 'The crag on the left… look up there…!'

Slowly unfurling on the breezy summit of the crag was a large white standard emblazoned with a golden dragon. Fellows found that his mouth was too dry to form a reply. Speechless for a moment, while he struggled to master the terror coursing through his veins, his entire being was screaming at him to take flight and get as far away as he could.

'It is the battle standard of Glendower,' Stone observed in an even, matter-of-fact voice. 'And there, if I am not much mistaken, is the man himself…'

Fellows spun around again and saw that the standard was still there but below the crag, riding a magnificent grey destrier, was a tall figure in full battle armour which shone brightly in the late afternoon sunlight. All Fellows saw, in his terror and excitement, was one man on a horse challenging him; he knew himself to be a novice, yes, but with a company of two hundred and fifty professional soldiers at his command. Giving voice to a hysterical laugh he drew his heavy sword, clutching at it desperately so that it would not fall and spoil his heroic appearance. He found himself shouting: 'All mounted men to me, to me.'

There were fifty mounted men at the head of the column. They had seen the armoured figure and needed little urging to join their leader. Fellows felt a great euphoria sweeping through him and, ignoring Stone's desperate shouts to stop, he dug his heels into the flanks of his horse, raised his sword and shouted: 'Charge!'

In seconds he, and at least fifty of his cavalry, were galloping towards the lone horseman to the consternation of his second in command and many other experienced officers and men. After the first hundred yards Fellows was already beginning to regret his hasty heroics. The sword was getting heavy and he tried to rest the blade across the back of the horse's neck. Then the world seemed to stand on its head as the low shrubs and bushes ahead all started to move, as if of their own accord.

Two rows of pikemen who had been well hidden behind the scrub materialised and formed up between the lone horseman and his attackers. The first row went down on one knee, digging the reverse ends of their pikes into the hard ground with the points aimed directly at the chests of the advancing horses. The second row remained standing, leaning forward on their pikes almost casually, ready to spear the mounted men. At the same time, scores of longbow men appeared from behind the crags and took up positions behind the pikemen, bows strung and arrows slotted at the ready.

Only too aware of the awesome power lined up against him, Fellows' nerve broke. Dropping his sword he raised his arm and screamed the order to halt. Unfortunately for him, he was the only one to attempt to do so. All the others, who had either misheard him, or realised that at twenty yards from the first row of pikemen it was too late to halt, kept going. As Fellows tried to stop his horse, the poor creature was buffeted from all sides by the other mounts careering on at the gallop and, in an instant, man and horse disappeared under scores of trampling hooves, condemned to a horrific death in a matter of seconds.

Few of the other riders realised what had happened, for at the same time the Welsh archers unleashed a deadly volley of arrows which, at a little over twenty paces, was lethal to man and beast. Horses and riders tumbled to the ground and the two rows of pikemen had only a ragged line of a dozen survivors to deal with as the dust cleared. The remnants, showing considerable courage, made straight for the pikemen and, within minutes, men and mounts had impaled themselves on the thick hedge of pikes. A sudden, unnatural silence followed the fatal charge as the Welsh contingent stared in disbelief at the destruction of life and limb all around them. The English, too, were frozen in horror as they saw Fellows and fifty of their number killed before their eyes. Roderick Stone shouted orders to the junior officers to close ranks and assume defensive positions, but before they could do so there came a baleful, booming noise from the valley as a horn sounded one long note. The doom-laden sound unsettled even the older, experienced soldiers. Before anyone had recovered, a hail of arrows came from the woods now some fifty yards to their left, followed quickly by another deadly volley. For a moment the sky went dark as a cloud of the projectiles tore at them like a swarm of wasps, then the air was rent with the shouts and screams of the injured and the dying, while many more keeled over and died without making a sound. One of these was Roderick Stone.

Panic reigned along the length of the column as

every able-bodied survivor sought whatever shelter they could find. Again the accuracy of the Welsh longbow men had taken a high toll, with more than thirty English soldiers killed and twice that number wounded, many seriously. Still they waited patiently for their orders, unaware that Stone was dead.

Back in the prisoners' wagon, Gwilym sprang into action. He had waited patiently for this moment – ever since he, and some of the other more quick-witted prisoners, had realised that Tom Easton was providing the double bluff which would spell disaster for his captors. Others had stared open-mouthed as understanding dawned that deliverance was at hand. But Gwilym knew they had to wait for the right moment to make their move. As he did so all their aches and pains fell away, replaced by an exciting surge of nervous energy.

Gwilym was urging Tom to take the keys away from the burly Harold, who was livid at the death of so many of his friends. He waved his arms in impotent rage and mouthed obscenities at the hidden archers in the woods. His garrulous companion, Alfred, was more concerned with saving his own skin and was crouched, trembling, behind one of the wagon's wooden wheels. Tom grabbed a piece of wood, normally used as a wedge for the wagon's wheels, and brought it down hard on Harold's head. The large man staggered but did not go down. He turned clumsily and, as his glazed eyes cleared, he saw Tom with the piece of wood, now dripping blood, in his hand. Understanding dawned slowly and Harold's little pig eyes changed from an expression of incredulity to one of fury.

'You,' he roared as his hand went up to his bleeding crown. 'It was you who led us into this trap, and now I'll kill you with me bare 'ands.'

Moving with surprising speed he jumped forward and gripped Tom's neck in both hands, intent on throttling him. Tom fought to free himself by kicking Harold's shins and clutching the irate guard's wrists to try and tear them away from his throat. He realised, immediately, that he had no chance. The man was as strong as an ox. As blackness descended he could hear the prisoners shouting, entreating him to fight back. He was losing consciousness and convinced that he was dying when Harold's body convulsed and his considerable weight came down on Tom, pinning him to the side of the wagon. His hands relaxed and fell away from Tom's bruised neck. With a low sigh Harold slid sideways and fell forward face down onto the ground. There was an arrow shaft embedded, deep in his back. The longbow men had released a third volley into the stricken English contingent bringing more death, pain and despair. Their nerve broken, the pitifully small band of survivors took to their heels and raced back down the path, leaving everything except the weapons in their hands. Alfred was the last, trying to run but only managing an awkward shambling trot. Despite his shouted pleas for help, he was soon left far behind by his fleeing companions. Finally he, too, disappeared around a bend and Gwilym, who had been sorely tempted to chase his former tormentor, decided that the pitiful creature was simply not worth the effort.

Scores of men now surged out of the woods shouting and calling to each other in celebration of their crushing victory. Releasing the prisoners was a slow job, for the irons in which they had been shackled were old and rusty. Finally, they were all able to stand and stretch their weary bodies and were mobbed by their delighted rescuers, most wearing the green jerkins of Glyndŵr though some were clad in light armour. There was a sudden call to order and the celebrations quickly stopped as two riders came thundering towards the wagons. One was the solitary man on the magnificent grey warhorse who had incited the first, disastrous charge led by Fellows. At his side was Rhys ap Tudur. Now, however, he had removed his armour and cut a dashing figure as he approached, clad in a surcoat emblazoned at front and back with the Prince of Wales' coat of arms, four lions rampant on a background of red and gold.

'It is Owain himself,' Gwilym ap Tudur informed

his fellows. 'And the horse is his famous steed, Llwyd y Bacsie, whose courage and devotion have saved our Tywysog in many a tight corner.'

The rider dismounted and strode towards them with a broad grin lighting up his face. At his approach, Gwilym ap Tudur went down on one knee and bowed his head. His men and Tom Easton immediately followed suit.

'Cousin Gwilym, gentlemen, please stand up. There is no call for ceremony on a battlefield.'

They all stood and Gwilym embraced his cousin enthusiastically. They were joined by Rhys ap Tudur and the two brothers embraced each other, both their faces flushed with relief. Tom, meanwhile, took the opportunity to study Glyndŵr, the man who had been the subject of so much discussion, praise and speculation over the past months. He was a tall, strong-looking man with a mane of tawny golden hair worn down to his shoulders in the old style. Although no longer regarded as fashionable, it was a style which suited him and added to his charisma. He sported a flowing moustache, with a fashionable forked beard covering the strong chin. Though big bodied, and easily a head taller than the six-foot Gwilym, he looked fit and trim with no obvious spare flesh. Tom had to admit that he was a handsome man. His mannerisms and the authority he exuded showed him to be a determined leader, used to being obeyed, but with a courtesy and respect for those around him which made it a pleasure to carry out his orders. His most memorable attribute, though, was his eyes. They were of an unusual, but striking, golden yellow colour and very expressive. They emphasised the warmth of his smile, adding a mischievous quality to it. Tom speculated, however, that they would probably take on a feral, cat-like quality when expressing anger. It was not difficult to understand how so many females from different walks of life had been mesmerised by him over the years. Below his left eye Tom noticed a small but distinctive mole. However, the only feature which confirmed him as a middle-aged man were the lines on his face and forehead, and even these added somehow to his personality and gravitas. Tom was startled to discover that Owain was meeting his gaze with a half-mocking smile.

'Well, Gwilym, before we secure the wagons and start the journey to our temporary base camp, I must meet the enigmatic Englishman who played such a major role in the success of our little adventure.'

'Of course. I'm sure you will find him a most pleasant and agreeable man.' Gwilym turned and motioned Tom to join them. 'Tonight, when we regale you with the details of our time in Conwy, you will hear how Tom, at first our unwilling prisoner, turned out to be one of our truest servants during the siege, not to mention his ideas and talents as a bowyer and fletcher which helped us so much.'

Glyndŵr ran his gaze over Tom and stroked his chin reflectively. 'Thomas Easton. I like to think that I am an open-minded man, but I have to tell you there is something about you and your new-found allegiance to our cause which does not quite add up. I like to know everyone around me, their loyalties, capabilities, motivations… that's it; I have still to understand what motivates you, a respectable English carpenter and fletcher, to espouse the cause of Welsh freedom from English rule. Even more perplexing is why you would submit to a most severe beating, bearing real and most painful injuries with fortitude, to betray and cause considerable deaths among your countrymen and loss of much-needed revenue to your King. However, I will give you every opportunity to convince me that my doubts are baseless. If you succeed, I shall offer you my most sincere apologies.'

'And if I don't succeed in convincing you…' Tom, though nonplussed by Glyndŵr's directness, gamely returned the suspicious stare with a tight smile, trying not to show his apprehension.

'If I am not convinced by the end of our discussions this evening, it can only mean that you are in Bolingbroke's pay.' There was a slight pause and Tom had a brief view of the icy, feral expression which he had previously imagined in the yellow eyes. 'Then you will know the full force of my anger.' The last words were said in a matter-of-fact whisper which chilled Thomas Easton to the core.

The tension was eased by Rhys Gethin who strode up to Glyndŵr with a new problem.

'Sire, the wagons are far too heavy and cumbersome to be drawn through the woods. The only ones we have a real interest in are the one carrying the tax revenues and the two containing provisions, which would be most welcome.'

'In that case the loads will have to be split into manageable parcels so that they can be carried by teams of men. I suggest we free the oxen from the wagon shafts so they can rest and forage for food. We must also send word to our supporters so that the animals and wagons can be distributed to loyal farmers in the area.'

With that, Glyndŵr mounted Llwyd y Bacsie and, motioning Gwilym, Tom, Rhys ap Tudur and Rhys Gethin to accompany him, led the way into the woods.

8

GLYNDŴR'S BASE CAMP for his fledgling army of five hundred men was situated in a large clearing in dense woodland, no more than five miles from the scene of the ambush. They had enlarged the clearing by cutting down saplings and branches of larger trees for use as makeshift poles, which formed the framework for crude huts roofed with piled fern. In the centre of this temporary 'village' stood a sturdy log structure, comprising a large central room, with several smaller sleeping quarters, a kitchen and a storeroom leading off it. It boasted a properly constructed thatched roof which would keep the indoor areas dry in the heaviest rain. There was a stone hearth in the middle of the central hall, with a small hole in the roof above it for smoke to escape. Small piles of logs had been placed in and around the hearth to dry, but there was nothing to suggest that a fire had yet been lit in it.

It was in the comparative comfort of the hall that the eight escapees and Tom dined on fresh bread, cawl and roast mutton, which proved the best meal they had savoured for many months. Their host had been joined by Rhys Gethin and two nobles from south-west Wales, Henry Dwn and Rhys Ddu. The south Walians spoke in the soft-accented Welsh of their homelands which Tom, Rhys Gethin and the Anglesey men had some difficulty in following. Likewise, the two southerners were sometimes perplexed by the odd word or expression uttered by the north Walians. Fortunately Owain, whose mother Elen was a native of Deheubarth, had no difficulty and acted as interpreter when required.

As soon as the meal was over and tankards had been suitably replenished with ale, Owain tapped the communal table.

'I feel sure that you would wish me to thank Morfudd the cook and her team for the delicious meal we have just shared. A meal of that quality is not often served up to soldiers in the field.' He waited a moment for the supporting chorus of thanks to die away.

'I have plans for carrying the fight to the English in all parts of Wales,' he began. 'I shall share some of the more immediate proposals with you presently. First of all, though, I shall refer to events, some of which the Conwy castle team may be unaware of. Afterwards, perhaps Gwilym will give us a flavour of life in Conwy over the last few months.'

'It will be my pleasure, cousin,' Gwilym responded with pride.

'Let us return for a moment to last September when

I was proclaimed Prince of Wales in Glyndyfrdwy.'
The golden yellow eyes sparkled with enthusiasm and
pride as he remembered that glorious event and the
jubilation of his family and closest followers. 'Many
have voiced surprise at the choice of date for that
historic day. Why start a rebellion with winter just
around the corner? Would it not have been better to
wait for the promise of spring? Well, several factors
forced me to declare myself when I did. You will know
that I have been in dispute with Reginald de Grey, Earl
de Ruthyn, for some years over a tract of my land which
he has occupied unlawfully. I have also been having
visits with increasing frequency from Uchelwyr from
far and wide who are extremely worried by a number
of developments, including Henry Bolingbroke's illegal
seizure of the English throne. Then, there are the new
and vicious laws introduced by Parliament, supported
by Bolingbroke, which ensure that all Welshmen are
relegated to a lowly status with virtually no rights in
their own country. As a people, we are left with neither
self-respect nor dignity, and no rights in law. This
means that an Englishman can treat a Welshman with
complete contempt without any means of redress.
Add to that the impossibly high taxes imposed by the
Lords in the Marches and by the King in the remainder
of Wales, and we are in a perilous position. We can
simply allow ourselves to disintegrate as a nation, or

stand and rebel against English rule, even though the odds are against us. We all have a great deal to lose and none more so than me. I had a large and loving family, a beautiful home, and though a Welshman, I was considered an aristocrat and a rich landowner. Now I, like all of you, am an outlaw with a price on my head. I still believe we chose the correct time to declare ourselves. Firstly, it was obvious that Henry saw us as a cow to be milked and there was no reason to believe that he would start showing us any kind of clemency or respect in the future. Secondly, he named his son, another Henry, as Prince of Wales.' A chorus of raised and angry voices greeted this announcement, for many in the company had not heard of this before.

'However, gentlemen, there is a third reason and this is the most compelling of all. At this moment, Henry the usurper is at his most vulnerable. His hold on the throne is weak. You see, there are many powerful men in England who do not support him and who do not believe he has a lawful right to the throne. He has to look over his shoulder all the time and accede to the demands of Parliament because he cannot afford to lose their support. Then, he has many enemies in neighbouring countries. The Scots, the Irish and the French would dearly love to destroy the power of England and Henry has to be ready to repel any attacks from the enemies beyond his borders. The last thing he needs is for us, the Welsh, to rise in rebellion, especially if we can rally country-wide support. I have to admit that we did not have a good start. A few days after our declaration on September 16th, I decided to give our friend Lord Grey a fright. With some two hundred and seventy men I attacked his home borough of Rhuthun, gathered the populace in the town square and set the place alight. Unfortunately, Grey was not at home. We then visited many other northern and Marcher towns and dealt them similar treatment.'

'We heard of your attacks on Rhuthun, Dinbych and Rhuddlan,' Gwilym interrupted. 'How many others were there?'

'We also plundered Flint, Hawarden, Holt, Oswestry and Welshpool. Then, on September 24th, our luck ran out. We met a much larger English force under Hugh Burnell who out-manoeuvred us, attacking us on two fronts at once. Fortunately it was in a valley with woods all around. There was no question of taking them on. We would have been massacred. I had to give the order for everyone to scatter and most of us managed to escape with our lives. We still lost two score of good men, though. Then Henry, thoroughly alarmed by our actions, brought a large army drawn from the men of ten English counties into north Wales. He marched along the coast to Bangor and Caernarfon, laying waste any Welsh settlements in his path. However, the men of Anglesey had risen in revolt and gave Henry quite a shock.'

Owain paused and smiled across the table at Gwilym and Rhys ap Tudur. 'The island rebels were led by the ap Tudur brothers. Tell us what happened next, Gwilym.'

'We realised that if the King came over to Anglesey he could only bring small detachments of his army across at any one time. This was because the Welsh vessels in the small Welsh ports along the coast had all put to sea to save being requisitioned by the King.' Gwilym looked around the room and grinned. 'We took full advantage of that and watched as the first few detachments were ferried across the strait from Bangor, and waited for Bolingbroke's arrival. After a few hours they had managed to land some three hundred men, and Bolingbroke himself finally arrived. Rhys and I were waiting for him with five hundred well-trained men. The English King found the situation too hot to handle and scurried over to Beaumaris to gain the protection of the castle. By the time he got there we had killed at least a hundred of his men and, King of England or not, he was forced to hide behind the walls of Beaumaris castle for several days. Eventually, a fleet of naval transports arrived in Bangor. He was able to get hundreds more men across quite quickly and we, now vastly outnumbered, returned inland and Henry wasted little time in departing the island which had given him such a fright.'

'Yes, and on reaching the mainland he turned south and completed his circuit of north Wales through Mawddwy and finally back to Shrewsbury, killing, burning homes, other buildings and crops as he went,' Owain concluded. 'In some ways it has to be said, his march around the north was successful. It resulted in a considerable number of those who had supported me initially seeking the King's pardon. My own brother, Tudur, was one and my old friend, Crach Ffinant the prophet and bard, was another.'

Gwilym and the other Anglesey men were quick to show their disgust at this news, banging the table and demanding to be heard.

'No, wait a moment, my friends. Let me finish. I can understand your anger and, believe me, I too was shocked initially on hearing the names of some of the defectors. Tudur, to be fair to him, did tell me face-to-face of his intention. He was simply not prepared to endanger his family and property. I was greatly saddened, however, that Crach, my old friend and comrade in arms, went to beg the King's pardon without saying a word about it to me.'

Owain waited again for the angry reaction to blow itself out.

'At least, I now know who my real, trustworthy

friends are. With winter approaching I sent all the men with families and holdings home, and they were relieved to hear that they could return to their folk, particularly as there would be no more significant military action until the spring. I was left with thirty or so hardened professional soldiers with few or no family ties, who had faced all the rigours of army life in other countries.

'We retired to an ancient fortress called Dolbadarn castle overlooking Llyn Peris in the heart of Snowdonia. It had originally been built in the sixth century and had been the home of the legendary Maelgwn Gwynedd. It was in rather a mess when we got there but we all worked like beavers to make it habitable. Most of the walls were in a fairly satisfactory state but we did have to roof the main hall and communal sleeping quarters, as well as the kitchens. We spent the first weeks collecting timber and thatching materials from valleys, some quite distant from that lonely place. Local people, too, were generous. Eventually we had completed the roofing and stacked a large supply of firewood for much-needed fires to keep us from freezing to death. My loyal band stayed with me, even though they knew I had no means of paying them during the winter. I have rewarded them by making them my elite personal guards. Henceforth, they will be known as Y Cedyrn and will carry my personal standard in battle, defending it with their lives. Now that summer is here we will embark on a campaign in mid and south Wales. We will attack castles and their English settlements to show Bolingbroke and everyone else that this is no failed local rebellion in north Wales, but a full-blown war in which we will draw support from throughout our land.'

Looking around at his cheering companions, Glyndŵr's face lost its smile as he noticed one member of the company sitting morosely, grim-faced and silent.

'Rhys Gethin.' Owain's voice pierced the cheers like a whiplash, and everyone fell silent. 'Rhys,' Owain began again in a more conciliatory tone, 'you do not join in your comrades' enthusiasm. Is there something troubling you?'

'I'm sorry, sire, but with all due respect, I do not see a reason for jubilation.' He paused, as if hesitating.

'You are among friends here, Rhys,' Owain said quietly. 'I would know what troubles you.'

'It has been more than eight months and what in God's name have we achieved? We have caused havoc in a number of towns which were poorly defended and we had to scatter when we first came up against a professional English force. I do not see what great things we will achieve by harassing the English with lightning raids, then vanishing again into woods or mountains. We need to build a really powerful army that can match the King head-on in battle if you are to be truly the Prince of all Wales!' Rhys Gethin's words came out in a rush reinforcing his frustration.

Several others started to argue with Rhys Gethin but Glyndŵr again raised his hand for silence.

'No. Wait. He does have a point. I agree that we will never defeat the English until we can put at least an equal number of soldiers in the field. Alas, we are not in a position to do that at present, and for the time being we must concentrate on what we do best – that is harrying, surprise attacks and using the mountainous terrain of Wales, and the weather too, to our advantage. We cannot match the enemy in numbers, in equipment, or in wealth to pay large army wages. However, being more lightly armed we are faster and more adaptable to fight in differing conditions, and we are good at what we do. Sadly, we will never be able to match the enemy in numbers. When I was studying law at the Inns of Court in London, I remember a wise old professor telling me that, for every Welsh person, there are twelve English people.'

He paused and studied the crestfallen faces.

'All I would ask is that you have faith in me. Do you really believe that in my middle years I would have given up my very comfortable existence as Lord of Sycharth and Glyndyfrdwy, my lands, my wealth and the pleasure of living in peace with my family, if I did not believe we could win this struggle? No, of course not. You see, I dream that one day Wales will be free once again to make its own laws, to have its own church, to be able to educate our young men in our own Welsh universities, one in the north, the other in the south. I also have plans to even up the numbers, so that we will be able to face the English in a fair fight. I am going to write letters to the kings of Scotland, Ireland and France – all enemies of Bolingbroke. I shall seek their support and invite them to send armies to assist us in our struggle.'

For a moment there was absolute silence. Henry Dwn, Rhys Ddu, and Rhys and Gwilym ap Tudur all stared at each other in amazement. Then they turned back to Glyndŵr, their admiration and respect for him mirrored in their eyes. They realised that this man was not just a war leader. Wales was blessed with a prince who was a thinker, a statesman even; and a strategist with a strong personality who was not afraid to hold discourse with some of the most powerful men in Europe. Here was an exceptional leader who would inspire loyalty and devotion in his followers. Even Rhys Gethin was smiling as he raised his tankard to his lips.

Feeling quietly satisfied with the warm response to his vision for Wales, Owain called upon Gwilym ap Tudur to relate the daring exploits of the men of Anglesey in capturing and holding Conwy castle for three months. Drawing gasps of admiration and amusement in turn, Gwilym regaled his listeners with his very personal and often exaggerated account of events at Conwy.

Finally, he turned to a relaxed and amenable prince and spoke in a more serious vein. 'Before I sit down, cousin, I would like to say a few words in support of an Englishman; not something I do every day of the week.' He waited while everyone, including Thomas Easton, laughed heartily at his wit. 'In all seriousness I would like you to know, Owain, that my brother Rhys and I will vouch for Tom's support for the cause and his loyalty to us all. We all know that Tom is English and would not wish to hide that fact. At the same time, he happens to be a good man, a fair man, and a loyal man. Since being forced to join us he has come to understand the injustices under which we labour and he is wholeheartedly behind us in our struggle to right the injustices being heaped upon us. He has proved this by being the best fletcher we have, and on more than one occasion he has risked his life to help us. One example is the way he endured much physical pain in order to look credible as the beaten up Englishman at the roadside, before succeeding in fooling Fellows and his escorting force about our plans. He willingly submitted to a very real and painful beating by Meurig ap Siôn, while two others held him by the arms.'

'But you said in your account that he and Meurig had become close friends,' Owain interrupted in astonishment.

'Precisely,' replied Gwilym. 'Meurig knew that if Fellows suspected, even for a moment, that Tom's story was not authentic, then he would be killed without compunction. Meurig's punches were intended to cause injury and hurt in order to keep him safe.'

'Yes, that was so good of him,' said Tom dryly in his best Welsh. 'I just hope that he will feel just as noble when I return the compliment, the next time we meet.' They all laughed at this and even Glyndŵr could not hide a broad grin.

'It would seem that despite my previous grave misgivings, Thomas Easton has been proved a resourceful and loyal supporter of our cause. Tom, it will be a pleasure to have you with us. I trust that you will join me and my small, but growing, army for our next campaign. Next week we march south, almost as far as Ceredigion, to set up a semi-permanent base camp on the deserted hills and moors of Pumlumon. From there we will begin the next stage of the war by raiding and firing the Anglo-Flemish boroughs of the south-west and laying siege to some of the key castles in the region. You can set off for Conwy tomorrow morning to relax in the company of your beloved Anglesey maid for a few days, before returning to join us for the march south. You may have to wait some time, though, before meeting your great friend Meurig ap Siôn, for he will be occupied in Anglesey and the north-west under the leadership of Rhys ap Tudur and Gwilym here, making a nuisance of themselves attacking more of the King's castles while we campaign in the south.'

Much later that night, when everyone had retired to their beds, a silent, shadowy figure emerged from the log building. He paused for a second, looking cautiously around for the sentries. He lifted his head as if sniffing the air like a hunted animal, then loped off barefooted, disappearing into the trees. The four sentries on perimeter guard heard nothing, for the silence of the warm summer's night had not been broken, apart from the occasional cheeping of bats hunting for insects in the still night air.

Rhys Gethin had been just twelve years old, living the only life he knew as a child of the hill people, when his mother told him that his father was Owain, of the aristocratic house of Powys Fadog. The hill people were remnants of the Brythonic peoples who had inhabited Britain from time immemorial, long before the Celts arrived. As a race they were small and dark. While most had eventually integrated into Celtic society, a few tribes had shunned the lifestyle of the newcomers, and even now lived by hunting and living off their wits in mountain fastnesses. Their homes were in caves and rudimentary shelters and their clothing still largely of animal skins. Most people gave them a wide berth, for although not normally hostile, they were redoubtable fighters and vicious when roused.

Trotting steadily northward on hard, calloused feet, Rhys recalled the moment when his mother's revelation had changed his life. From then on, all the boy could think of was his close relationship to the 'other' people, and especially that he was the son of a nobleman. In 1392, at the age of sixteen, he was developing into a wiry, if rather thin young man, and one day he told his mother that he would go in search of his father to let the great lord know that he had another son. Initially, his mother had expressed alarm and warned him that Owain would not welcome this news. Later, having reflected on the matter, she began to think of the positives of such an action. She still remembered the kindness and gentle manners the young Owain had shown towards her during their short period as lovers. If Rhys were to be accepted by his father, it could lead to a much better life for the son she cherished.

One morning the young boy had arrived at the gates of Sycharth and demanded to meet Owain Glyndŵr. The guard had brusquely dismissed him, but the boy refused to leave. The guard threatened him with a good whipping if he did not leave. Fortunately Maredudd,

Owain's second son, who was of the same age, heard the guard shouting and was impressed by the ragged boy's courage and determination in defying the command to leave.

'No, Eryl, don't send the lad away. Let him in, if you please. I shall answer for it.'

'Are you sure you know what you are doing, young Maredudd? These people are not to be trusted in civilised households. As for meeting your father – what could he possibly have to say to a nobleman, like your father?'

'We'll soon find out, won't we?' Maredudd grinned at Rhys.

The disgruntled Eryl had reluctantly opened the gate, making no secret of his disapproval. Maredudd had led Rhys Gethin into the family quarters where his parents were having breakfast. He could not hide his admiration for the hill boy, fascinated by the long dagger in his belt and the roughly-made longbow and quiver of arrows carried over his shoulder.

'What is your name?'

'I am called Rhys. Rhys Gethin.'

'I have to ask you to leave your weapons outside. Nobody carries arms into my father's quarters.'

The boy scowled and stopped. 'I always carry my weapons wherever I go,' he said obstinately.

'Don't worry, Rhys. I shall get a trusted servant

to look after them for you. You can have them back as soon as you leave my father's quarters, I promise,' Maredudd said patiently.

For a moment it seemed the boy would refuse. He ran his fingers through his tousled hair uncertainly, and sighed before capitulating. 'They will be safe?' he asked in a small voice.

Maredudd warmed to him as the child within the lad showed through briefly. 'On my honour. They will be perfectly safe.'

Maredudd knocked and entered the room. Mared, Owain's wife, was eating oat cakes and drinking milk, while Owain was doing justice to a large plate of bread and cheese with a tankard of small beer to drink.

'Ah, Maredudd. Up early this morning, I see,' Owain greeted his son affably.

'Bore da Mam, Nhad.' Maredudd hesitated, looking at his mother. Mared was tall and dark-haired and thoroughly devoted to her husband and large brood of children. Though not pretty in a conventional sense, she was attractive and graceful with a ready smile, and well liked and respected by everyone at Sycharth. Yr Arglwyddes was how everyone at Sycharth always referred to her.

'What is it, Maredudd?' she asked. 'You sound a bit unsure of yourself.'

'Well, it's just that Father has an unexpected visitor.

A young lad about my age came to the gate asking to speak to you, Father. The guard turned him away but he refused to leave. Well, I liked the way he stood up to Eryl, the guard, who was threatening him with a whipping, so I asked him in.'

'Did you now… do you know anything about him, or what he wishes to speak to me about?'

'No, only that by his appearance I think he is of the hill people.'

Owain frowned, stroking his beard thoughtfully. Then, his face lighting up in a smile, he said, 'I suppose you had better invite him in so we can hear what he has to say.'

A moment later Maredudd led Rhys into the room. The boy was trying hard to hide his nervousness as he stood to attention, feet set slightly apart. He stared longingly at the table. Seeing the well-stocked breakfast table made him feel ravenous.

'I am Owain Glyndŵr. I understand you wish to speak with me.'

'Yes, sire. My name is Rhys Gethin and what I have to say is for your ears alone.'

'Have no fear, Rhys Gethin. We have no secrets here and you can speak freely before Yr Arglwyddes and Maredudd.'

'Are you sure, my lord?'

'Perfectly sure.'

'I am of the hill people, sire, and my mother tells me that I am your son.'

Mared paled for a moment, then her cheeks flamed in embarrassment. Maredudd's face initially registered shock which was quickly replaced by embarrassment.

'You will excuse me if I leave now,' Mared murmured in a low voice. 'I have better things to do than listen to this nonsense.' She rose abruptly and left the room, but not before both Owain and the two boys had noticed her lower lip quivering and her eyes welling up with tears.

Maredudd also turned to leave.

'No, Maredudd. I want you to stay. You are now an adult and I want you to hear everything.' He turned to Rhys Gethin. 'What is your mother's name?'

'She is called Mabli.'

Owain stared at the boy for a long time as if seeking a reflection of himself in the lad's eyes. Rhys stared back unflinching, with only a slight tapping of an index finger on his leather belt betraying his nervousness.

At last Owain sighed and smiled kindly at Rhys. 'I have nothing apart from your mother's word to indicate that you are my son. I did indeed have a... er... close friendship with someone called Mabli, and she was of the hill people. We eventually went our separate ways, for there was no future for our friendship. However, she never gave me an inkling by word or deed that she was with child.'

'Sire. When I told my mother that I was going to tell you how I am your son, she was much alarmed. She thought you would find the news unwelcome.'

A shadow of sadness flitted briefly across Owain's countenance. 'I can believe it. She would never knowingly be the cause of trouble or heartache to me. I am afraid I cannot recognise you as my son, for I will never know for sure whether you are or not. But this is what I will do. I will provide you with a home here in Sycharth for as long as you wish. For that, you will have to agree to be educated in Welsh and in English and be trained as a squire, so that you will always be aware of the ways of civilised men and how to behave in such company. I will also train you in the use of weapons.'

'I already know how to use weapons,' said Rhys haughtily.

Owain smiled. 'Well, if you do, that will mean less work for me. If, as I suspect, your knowledge of weapons is rudimentary, then you will marvel later at how much you did not know, and one day you will thank me. Now, you must seek your mother's permission if you are to live here with us. But before you go, Maredudd will take you to find some breakfast. Cook will take one look at your skinny frame and give you the biggest plateful you have ever seen, boy. Off with you…'

As he continued his progress swiftly and silently through the woods, Rhys smiled as he remembered the tremendous difficulties Glyndŵr had faced in his efforts to educate and civilise him. The boy from the hills had never overcome his aversion to living and sleeping within four walls and, while he grew to understand the protocols, customs and behaviours of 'civilised society', he never accepted them completely. Consequently, he would disappear for days to his mountainous home and live with the hill people, only to return eventually, surrendering to the inevitability of a compulsory bath and change to 'normal' clothing. Even now, nine years later, he was not totally accepted by everyone at Sycharth and people there had recognised that there was a part of Rhys Gethin which would never be tamed.

Soon the tangled undergrowth gave way to larger, more solitary trees, spaced apart so that the strong moonlight shone through, making everything clearly visible but coated in silvery shadow which gave off a strange, unearthly ambience. Rhys was no longer smiling and had slowed to a walk. Finally he stopped and slowly discarded his clothing. Then, stark naked, he entered a large clearing where a huge, ancient

Also in the series:

£7.99

oak stood in stately isolation at its centre. He pause
reverentially, then moved forward with slow, deliberate
steps until he stood directly beneath the massive old
tree. As he looked up through its canopy, slivers of
bright moonlight sliced through gaps in the leafy
branches, creating small pools of light about his bare
feet. With a deep sob, Rhys stretched out his arms and
clutched as much as he could of the oak's holy trunk.
He felt the hard ridges of the gnarled bark against his
flesh, silently commanding him to raise his gaze. Then,
he lifted his head and howled like a dog in supplication
to the moon goddess.